# HELL ON MARS

## REALITY BLEED

J.Z. FOSTER

JUSTIN M. WOODWARD

WINTER GATE PUBLISHING

*In memory of Tonya Renee Woodward and all those who have been lost to cancer.*

*You are gone but not forgotten.*

# PROLOGUE

THE FELICITY STATION on Mars was running on minimal life support and emergency services only. Batteries powered it for now, and they too would eventually die. The main power had been killed, cutting off energy to all nonessential functions.

That included the gate.

*We tore a hole in reality.*

That thought reverberated through Will Braun's mind. They'd been so eager with their experiments, with contacting things on the other side.

They'd powered the gate, just as they had been directed.

And something horrible came through.

*Alien? . . .Demon?*

Each was a thought in Braun's head. Each a theory that needed to be weighed and tested, but he was having trouble focusing.

"*Scheisse*," Braun whispered, reverting to German. It was a habit he had yet to drop.

The emergency lights continued to silently flash throughout the facility, and each flash illuminated the thing in the hallway.

The thing that used to be a man.

It stared at them—those few to have survived—and though it didn't speak, they all understood.

It wanted them.

It had a name once—Mark Rufus—but it showed little of Rufus now. Just the shell and the skin atop it.

Will Braun himself was little of a man anymore, but at least he still thought like one. As much as he ever had anyway.

Curious, Braun noticed the creature had little regard for its own health as it slammed its hands against the thick glass embedded in the security door. Of course, Braun couldn't hear it, but somehow his mind still imagined the sounds of the *thud* as its fist hit and the *crack* as the small bones in its hand broke.

There were few things that Will Braun was thankful for, but at the moment, the thick glass in each of the doors of Mars' Felicity station was one of them.

Rufus, Braun's friend—if he'd ever had any friends at all—had a child and an ex-wife on Earth. Not that he had ever told Braun, as they spent little time discussing trivial details when their work was of such importance. Braun only knew that because he'd seen the accounting records with the remittance stipulated *child support*. But the thing staring at Braun from behind the glass with hungry eyes was no longer Rufus.

It wasn't even a man anymore. He had to remember that.

Braun too had shed most of the mortal coil but in a far slower process. His uncombed gray hair and the patch of flesh above his jaw were nearly all that remained of the body his mother had given him.

The rest he'd received from the U.S. taxpayers.

What he'd lost from age and disease had been replaced to keep him fully functioning. Mechanical eyes twisted and focused. There was an engine in the hollow spot of his chest where his heart had been—it kept the blood flowing. All of this because he was a mind unlike any other. A mind with vision and dreams rarely seen.

And here was what had become of that vision.

*We heard a knock.*

Braun remembered Rufus telling him that. Back when Rufus was a man and not the monster behind the glass. Back when Rufus's eyes filled with wonder and excitement and not a haunting call for flesh.

*We heard a knock. Something is listening.*

The thing that had once been Rufus heaved onto the glass, fogging it. Its eyes had yellowed, and quivering black thorn-like whiskers had sprouted through its cheeks. Long, reaching insectile legs had erupted from its back. Its jaw rattled and quivered with anticipation and hunger as it clawed at the glass.

Looking back now, Braun knew they had been too eager, too interested in the unknown and the unstudied. A new frontier had opened up before him, one upon which no other man had seen.

*"Think about what we can do,"* Olivia Lewis, a station director, had said, her eyes shining like a child with a new toy.

*Children. New toys. That's what we were.*

Now Lewis was dead. Likely anyway. He hadn't seen it happen, but he knew she wasn't here now. She was somewhere *there*, on the other side of the door—the door between him and the thing that had once been Mark Rufus.

Possibly eaten by Rufus himself.

Rufus had been decent once—he did what he was told and rarely complained. Braun had to remember that. It was hard with Rufus beating against the glass, one of his eyes crushed and hanging by its optic nerve, to remember that the thing had once been a person.

Braun watched him—*it*—curiously. It was strange because he couldn't hear anything from Rufus. He couldn't hear the groaning from Rufus's lips, or the snap as—just now—his wrist broke against the glass and left a red smear. It elicited a new round of screams from the others in Braun's room—colleagues who had been lucky enough to make it here.

Braun turned from Rufus—there was little else to learn from the frantic raging of a clearly insane entity—and Braun's mechanical eyes began to whirl and click in his head, an annoyance he'd long become accustomed to hearing.

"What are we going to do?" asked a woman with tears flowing down her face.

He ignored her as he counted. There was little use in engaging in hysterics.

*Twenty.*

That's how many had survived of a working crew of approximately one hundred and fifty souls.

*Twenty. Approximately fourteen percent. Leaving approximately eighty-six percent presumed dead.*

"What the hell were those?" an old balding man with graying hair asked. Leonard. Braun only knew him in passing. He wasn't in any of Braun's research departments. It must have been particularly startling for him when the gate opened. At least Braun was aware of where the things had come through.

"That remains unclear," Braun said with the tone of a man working his way through a particularly complex math equation.

*Human? Clearly not. Infected? Near certainty. Infection transmission possibilities? Direct contact? Certain. Indirect contact? Uncertain. Airborne particles?*

Braun stopped, pausing mid breath as he looked around the room. A small group of huddled survivors were, by all appearances, uninfected. They were possibly all that remained of the staff on Mars Felicity Station.

*Airborne particle transmission unlikely. Symptoms of infection?*

He looked once more to Rufus as he bellowed and smashed a broken wrist into the glass.

*Ravenous. Aggressive. Insane.*

Another thought came into his mind. He had watched something terrible tear apart and devour a young research assistant. Her screams revealed a grim fact: they did not wait until she had died.

*Hungry.*

Once more he looked amongst the men and women in his room, and once more he considered.

*Infected member within group? Possible to likely. Clear ability to determine? Direct to undress and inspect for wounds. Group likelihood of submitting to instructions? Unlikely. Reasonable to proceed? Yes.*

"Everyone," Braun said, his voice filled with determination and focus. "Undress. Right now. We need to see if anyone has been wounded."

"What the hell are you talking about?" Leonard asked, sweat dripping down his face as he breathed. "Someone better tell me what the hell is going on! Those . . . things out there, they—they ate my—"

*Best course of action? Confront and subdue Leonard.*

"—whole research team! They came screaming into my lab and—"

"An experiment," Braun interrupted. He walked toward Leonard. "A *failed* experiment."

Leonard focused on Braun, confusion turning toward hate. "What kind of—"

"A gate." Braun's voice was cold and emotionless. "Something was on the other side. It talked with us and—"

"*You* did this?" Leonard screamed so loudly his glasses nearly fell off. He shoved them back up his nose, and then thrust a finger at Braun. "*You*—"

*Tactics failing. Increase aggression.*

Braun stepped closer, forcing Leonard's finger to poke him in the chest. Another step forward and Leonard backpedaled.

"Shut your mouth and listen to me or you're dead." Braun broke eye contact with Leonard to look across the room, making sure everyone felt the force of his presence. "Everyone, quiet. This is not the time for hysterics."

"Are they aliens?" someone shrilled. Braun didn't see who.

"What you see at the door?" Braun pointed at Rufus. "No, he was one of us. Now he is, perhaps, infected."

"*Perhaps?*" another said.

"Yes. Perhaps."

Leonard turned to face the crowd. "Then we need to—"

"Listen to me," Braun interrupted. "*Everyone* listen to me. Whatever they once were, they are no longer human and should not be treated as such. Most likely, he—" Braun pointed at Mark Rufus just as he screamed at the window. "—is infected. The most likely possibility is through direct contact or wounding from another infected. It's paramount now that you all undress and be inspected for wounds."

5

"And then what?" Leonard asked, his tone finally indicating capitulation.

Braun paused, looking to his personal research assistant, Tonya Foulks. He didn't need to ask the question.

"The power was cut, and the gate is now off. There aren't any more coming through. However, we believe the communication has failed," Tonya said. A bead of sweat rolled down her face, and she pushed her black glasses up on her nose again. "Earth didn't get the signal."

"It won't matter," Braun said. "When we go dark, they'll send a team to find out why. It'll be some time before the team shows up. We'll wait for them in cryo." No one disagreed as he moved to his cryo bed, preparing to sleep until help arrived. "The poor bastards." He glanced back at Rufus, and mumbled to no one in particular. "They won't have any idea what they're getting into."

---

## 1

COMMANDER JAMES TEALSON leaned out of bed and rolled his neck, stretching his tight muscles.

*"After extended cryosleep, two hours of daily exercise are recommended to avoid injury,"* the sweetly feminine A.I.'s voice reminded him as soon as it detected he had awakened.

"Yeah. To hell with that." He blinked and yawned. Three nights into sleeping on a bed and he was still feeling the effects of the long cryosleep. It hit everyone differently, some worse than others. Tealson had mild stomach pain, but Paxton George, the ship's data technician, spent more time sitting on the can than he did at his module. Mostly, Tealson was just foggy and sore. "Two hours my ass," he mumbled.

He made his way to his private bathroom—a privilege of being the *Perihelion's* captain—and relieved his bladder. His stomach gurgled.

"Fucking cryo."

He shouldn't have had to go into cryosleep. The crew was scheduled for a cargo run to the joint U.S. and European Federation Space Station, when the order came down from Orbital Corps.

*REASSIGNED. MARS FELICITY STATION WITHOUT COMMUNICATION. DETERMINE CAUSE AND REPAIR EQUIPMENT.*

Three weeks of vacation were washed away with one simple command statement.

Go-boys. That's all he and his crew were.

He huffed as he finished in the bathroom and made his way to his dresser, fitting his jacket on with all the pretty little insignias of rank. He didn't bother to button it all the way up, as per regulation. Few bothered with regulation when they're seven months away from Earth and dealing with constipation from being stuck too long in the freezer.

He grabbed his pack of cigarettes off his desk, a blank silver packaging with a single candy cane stripe around it indicated the peppermint taste. They called them candy cane cigs. Tealson had found it in the back of a cabinet in the breakroom and taken it, a total desperation move. His own supply of cigarettes had run dry a week before entering cryo. Another casualty of being reassigned with extended service mid-run, he didn't have a chance to resupply. It was likely someone else's on the ship who tried to hide it rather than get it confiscated for breaking regulations. Whoever it belonged to would likely notice that their pack was missing and Tealson smelled like candy cane cigs, but hell with it. Smoking was bad for you, wasn't it?

*Yep. Did them a favor.*

He chuckled at the thought.

If there was no one on Mars who could hook him up with a pack of reds, he might have to go hunt in the cargo load and blame it on rats.

*Rats, sir! Big ass ones that like to smoke!*

The thought made him grin as he walked toward the bridge, popping a cigarette into his mouth as he entered.

"Morning," Bennie Halsworth, the ship navigator, said from his booth. "Don't think that cig is regulation, Commander."

"Neither is that mop of hair, Halsworth." Tealson plopped into his seat and pulled a lighter from his pocket. "Come talk to me after you get a haircut."

"Whoa, man," Bennie said, folding his arms in front of his chest. "Halsworth is my father, thank you very much."

Tealson shot a glance at Bennie. "What was all that about regulation, again?" He lit the cigarette and took a puff.

Sweet candy cane peppermint filled his lungs as he typed his credentials into the module. He winced at the taste and pulled the cig out, considering again if it was even worth it. Defeated, he put it back in his mouth.

He opened up a command screen to see if Mars had been able to signal them, a near-futile hope that the problem might be solved before they arrived. His hopes were dashed when he saw there still hadn't been any communication. "They're holding that goddamn place together with duct tape," he mumbled under his breath, the cigarette dangling between his lips.

Bennie nodded as he yawned in his seat. He leaned back and scratched his bearded cheek. "Sooner or later, they're just going to have to pull the plug and let it all go dark. Waste of tax dollars."

Tealson shook his head and took another drag. "No, they'll keep it for as long as the lights stay on. It's a perpetual middle finger to the Russians. *Look what we did that you couldn't.*"

"Goddamn Russians." Bennie hissed out a breath. "You hear they shot down Concord six eleven?"

"What the hell is Concord six eleven?"

Bennie tilted his head. "The passenger plane? It was privately owned and flying near Vietnam's air space?" He leaned forward to his terminal and scrolled. "Been reading all about it. They're trying to say it was some hill boys in Vietnam, like those goddamn Russians weren't supplying them anyway. Just like those Comanche that gassed those kids in Colorado. Anyway, those assholes are trying to say it was filled with CIA operatives and not just some rich assholes blowing through their money."

"You know it was probably some fucking CIA spooks, right?"

"That's not what I read. I read that—"

"I don't read that shit anymore," Tealson said flippantly.

"You don't read the news anymore?"

"Hell no I don't, and you shouldn't either, Bennie. It's all *starving Japanese deserters shot at the DMZ, radiation deaths in Germany rising for the seventh consecutive year,* and *European Federation in continued negotiations with the US over bailout package."* Just talking about it made Tealson's pulse quicken. "It's enough to make me want to hang myself."

"Might want to wait until you get home. Could be hard to do with only eighty-five percent gravity."

Tealson snorted. "That some kind of joke?"

"Just saying. Besides, it won't be too long before we put you out to pasture anyway."

"Nope, not too long at all." There, that was something to look forward to. A nice long retirement where he could bury his head in the sand and try to forget all about the Russians and their nukes. "Counting the months down, let me tell you."

But was he? After Jennifer got remarried and changed her name to Wilson, something about keeping his feet on the ground tasted a little more sour.

*Jennifer Wilson. Well, hope she's happier now.*

"I'm sure you are," Bennie said. "Hell, I'm just waiting until this tour is over. I'd like a nice, long stint back on Earth. Been a while since I crapped in a gravity drop toilet."

"The fact that you call it a gravity drop toilet and not just a *toilet* makes me think you're enjoying yourself out here a little too much."

Bennie stood up and stretched. "Well, gravity drop toilet or not, nature calls."

"Have fun." Tealson threw a wave up over his shoulder as Bennie left.

*Bennie and his gravity drop toilet. A sure sign of a man who has spent too much time in space. But what about me? What the hell am I going to do planetside? Burying my head in the sand is only fun for so long.*

That had always been the dream. Work an honest job for as long as he was required by Orbital Corps before being allowed to retire with full benefits. Cargo run after cargo run until the Corps said, "That's enough. You can go home." He was such a pessimist these days, so it was hard to get excited about anything, even retirement. What was he supposed to do after he retired? *Take up golf?* Truth was, he didn't know what he wanted. But it sure as hell wasn't *golf.*

He hissed loudly and took another puff. He'd sooner smoke himself to death than head out onto the course with a goofy-ass pair of pants.

If he wanted to try and relax, he should take a cue from one of the newest crewmen, Tommy Reeves. Reeves was excited to be going to Mars, and he didn't even try to hide it.

*Maybe the trip would be a breath of fresh air?*

"Nice, recycled air," he said out loud.

"What's that, Commander?" came a voice from behind Tealson, causing him to jump a little. Turning, he saw their pilot, Linda Stalls.

"Shit, nothing. Just passing the time." He took one last drag and stubbed his cigarette into a nearby ashtray.

"Coffee's ready." She thumbed behind her as she planted herself into a seat, her fingers instantly going to pick at a tear in the cushion.

"Fantastic," Tealson said, only half as enthusiastic as he seemed. He did enjoy a good cup of coffee after all, even if it did come from a labelless, metal canister. "At least you had something to do since you sure as hell aren't flying this thing."

"Very funny," Stalls said. "Just remember that when I land this bird safely on that rusty rock. Unless you'd rather give it a shot?"

"Only if you take my job," Tealson quipped and got out of his seat, following the smell of fresh coffee. "Come on, you don't have anything better to do. Let's go on a walk and see about those two hours of exercise."

"Sure." Stalls got up to follow him. "And what is it exactly that you do, anyway?"

"Watch it, Stalls," Tealson said with a smirk. "Or I really will take you up on your offer to land this thing. Hell, who knows? Maybe I'm good at it."

She stood up and followed him into the ship's small galley, and Tealson grabbed one of the cheap metal mugs to pour himself a cup. Taking a sip, he winced and said, "They extend our mission by fourteen months, and still all they stock us with is this dirt coffee."

"*Yeah*," Stalls groaned. "They keep the dirt coffee well stocked. I'm with you, though, I had to cancel my vacation with my sister. You know they probably have this place bugged or something. Hear us bitch too much, and they tack on another tour."

Tealson set his coffee down. "I don't know. Maybe it's good to get out here and stretch our legs. Beats cargo runs, I suppose. Will be the first time I get to see the inside of Felicity station."

"Really? I thought you said you've done a few cargo runs to Mars?"

"Yeah, and the bastards always stop you in the docking bay." Tealson grinned, remembering about ten years back when a dockhand was paying under the table for *Playboy* magazines. Porn was worth its weight in gold when you lived on Mars.

Stalls smirked. "What are you smiling about?"

Tealson waved her off.

Just then Bennie popped his head into the doorway. "Um, Commander, the, uh. . . the shitter's broken again."

Tealson put his face in his palm. "I thought I told you to have the kid look at it?" He snapped his fingers, seemingly lost in thought with a pained expression on his face. "What's his damn name?"

"Burns?" Stalls suggested.

"That's it."

"Yes, sir," Bennie said. "I had Burns take a look, but all he said was —and I quote—'I'm a duties officer, not a space plumber.'"

Tealson grunted. "Of course he did. Let me finish my coffee and I'll take a look."

## 2

ALICE WINTERS ROLLED off Tommy Reeves, brushing a sweaty strand of hair behind her ear. They always finished with her on top, and each time, Tommy leaned back and closed his eyes. The napping type. It was bad enough having to keep quiet on the ship, but Tommy trying to pass out without at *least* spraying himself off?

"You're disgusting," she laughed.

He kept his eyes closed. "And yet you keep sleeping with me."

"You're really just going to roll over and take a nap? Come on, you're not a high schooler. Go wash yourself off and brush your teeth."

Tommy laughed. "I'm good."

"See? This is why we always fuck in your bed." She got up and walked toward the bathroom, knowing that Tommy would be watching her. He only pretended to sleep until she got up and walked away. "I don't want your nasty ass on mine."

She glanced back to see him staring at her. "Predictable." She grinned.

"What is?" Tommy asked, smiling but confused.

As Alice walked into the bathroom, the lights came on automatically and the A.I. system began speaking in a sweet, feminine voice.

*"After extended cryosleep, two hours of daily exercise are recommended to avoid injury."*

"Two hours a day?" Tommy called from the bed. "How long was that? Thirty minutes? Think you can go two or three more times?"

She laughed as she grabbed her toothbrush and squeezed on a layer of toothpaste. "Maybe." She peeked out to see Tommy staring out the windows toward the stars. She thought it was kind of cute, the way he was still interested in the stars after all this time traveling in space.

She stuck the brush in her mouth. "But you're going to have to brush your teeth first." She started scrubbing.

"What the hell is it with you and wanting to brush your teeth after sex? Want that skanky taste of my tongue out of your mouth?"

She spit in the sink and leaned out to point her toothbrush at him. "Don't think you're kissing me until you brush your teeth."

Tommy tucked his hands behind his head. "That's the problem with letting a lady keep a brush in your place. She's going to start demanding you brush your teeth more. I half think you're only banging me to use my bathroom."

She scrubbed her teeth while looking into the mirror, then spit again and said, "Definitely doesn't hurt your chances of getting laid. It is a little ridiculous that there are only three rooms with private bathrooms on this ship and the electrical engineer randomly gets assigned one."

"If you can't be good, be lucky, babe." Tommy smiled smugly.

Alice glanced out once more to see him still staring out the window. She rolled her eyes and rinsed her toothbrush. She stepped into Tommy's shower and washed herself off. It made her laugh to think about how much Tommy loved the stars. She'd gotten over those big balls of gas faster than the fact that she showered with recycled bathroom water.

"Perfectly clean," Cameron Elliot had assured her months ago. "The only problem is that mental hurdle you need to jump over—that it's the same water we flush down the toilet."

*"Yeesh,"* she groaned as she turned the water off, her skin suddenly

covered in goosebumps. Maybe she wasn't entirely over it after all. It was her first time on an extended run like this. Tommy's too. They were among the few new recruits added to the *Perihelion* for the Mars mission. She had of course been on many deployments as a combat medic, but never anything this far-reaching.

She toweled herself off and looked into the mirror. She grinned at her reflection and ran a hand through her blonde hair. She sure as hell didn't want to walk through the ship with sex-hair. Satisfied, she walked back in, looking for her clothes.

"You know, this will be my first time on Mars," Tommy said, grinning and moving past her to the bathroom.

"Oh, I know. You've told me." She found her underwear and tossed the towel aside as she pulled them up her hips. "You know it's just a big ugly rock, right?"

"That's your problem. You think everything is ugly."

She walked into the bathroom. "I don't know about that. I like this all right." She slapped his ass. "It's the real reason why I'm sleeping with you. The shower is just a bonus." She laughed and hugged him from behind, pressing her breasts into his back and placing her chin on his shoulder. "You're cute, but heading out there to fix a base that was built thirty years ago sounds more like a pain in the ass than a vacation."

He rubbed the fog off the mirror and looked at her reflection. "How many guys get to say they slept with a chick on Mars? It'll make for a great story. We'll see if we can turn the gravity down to just twenty percent."

She rolled her eyes.

He grabbed his own toothbrush and squeezed a layer of toothpaste onto it. "I can't believe you're not more excited. Isn't it fun going to someplace you've never been? I mean, we're talking about a whole *planet*, Alice."

"You know we're not going to be doing any sightseeing, right? We've got a few more weeks before we land. There's at least a possibility they signal us saying everything is all rosy, and we're cleared to turn around and go back."

"Shit, I hope not."

She grinned, watching him in the mirror. "You know, if we keep this up, I'm going to have to move my lotion in here." She rubbed his shoulders gently.

"So you're into private bathrooms and think Mars is just a big orange rock." He stuck his toothbrush into his mouth and started to scrub. He spit then said, "Makes me wonder why you're even in Orbital Corps."

The question peeled the smile off her face. She leaned off him and went to pick up her shirt.

"What?" He glanced at her as he scrubbed and then spit again. "What'd I say?"

"Nothing." She put her bra and shirt on and walked to a nearby mirror, glancing at her hair and shrugging before deciding to pull it into a messy bun.

He gargled some water and spit it out. "Wait a second, you're going to have to give me a little more than that." He set his toothbrush down and wiped his face on a towel.

"No, it's fine. I've just got shit to do."

"Oh come on, I'm sorry, I didn't mean to—"

"It's just personal, okay," she said with more bite than she meant to. "Don't worry about it." She grabbed a pair of pants from the edge of the bed and slipped into them.

"Yeah, sure." Tommy walked in to face her. "Listen, it's not exactly an original story. Lots of people join the Corps to get away from the bullshit. It's hard to find drama out here in the stars, right?" He turned to look out again.

"Oh, shut up." She rolled her eyes and mocked him, "*Out here in the stars!* You sound so stupid. How can you keep doing that? They're just big balls of gas. Like a space fart that you keep staring at."

He snorted and laughed. "Shit, you're hilarious."

"You're sweet. A little stupid, but sweet," she teased.

"This from the chick who voluntarily chooses to go to space but hates every minute of it."

She took in a deep breath and let it out slowly. "I wouldn't say I hate *every* minute of it." She leaned in and kissed him. He wrapped an arm around her.

"Oh, I'm loving *every* minute of it." He squeezed her ass.

She giggled. "You looking to get in some more exercise already?"

"Hey, if all it takes to get you hot is brushing my teeth, I'm game."

# 3

"YOU BEGGING US AGAIN, KID?" Tommy Reeves said, raising his eyebrows as he sipped water from a metal cup. He had to admit, Mike Burns, the duties officer, was hilarious in a stupid kind of way. Tommy guessed he weighed about a hundred and fifty pounds, and looked every bit the fresh faced new recruit.

"I'm just sayin'," Burns said, holding his hands out. "Nothing better to do, right?"

Tommy snorted and grinned at Alice. This was probably the third time Burns had brought up strip poker this week. Whenever two of the ladies happened to be in the galley at once, Burns would start pulling out his cards. "Kid is just dying to see your tits, Winters."

"It's not happening, Burns." Alice made a face and shook her head. "I'm not in college anymore."

"It's not like that!" Burns scowled. "It's just fun, right? Nothing else to do on this stupid ship."

Joseph DalBon, the crew's flight engineer, laughed loudly, his belly shaking beneath his uniform. "Kid, when was the last time you shaved?" He picked a chip out of a bowl and tossed it into his mouth.

"Why do you all keep calling me 'kid'? Shit's annoying." Burns puckered up his face.

"Bet he doesn't shave," Stalls said as the machine filling her bottle dinged. She came over to take a seat. "Right, Burns?"

"Shave my balls." Burns shot back. "Use his razor too." He pointed across the table at DalBon.

DalBon slapped the table. "Good one! Be careful though, kid. One slip and you'll take those little nuggets clean off." Everyone laughed, and Burns slumped into his seat. "Eh, don't worry about it. I don't shave either. Lets the women know you're fertile. The razor's just for my neck because I'm not a goddamn savage."

"You got cards?" Stalls asked Burns. "I'm game. Winters, Reeves, you in?"

Alice grinned at Tommy, and he nodded. Alice said, "If Stalls's in, so am I."

Burns's eyes went wide as the gravity of the situation became clear. Tommy laughed again and said, "Me too. Why not? DalBon's always trying to see my dick since I don't share a shower with the men anyway."

DalBon rolled his head back and laughed. "Well, it wouldn't be fair if I wasn't dealt in, would it?"

"Like anyone wants to see your fat ass," Burns said as he dug out his cards.

"Oh, spicy." DalBon looked at Stalls. "You think I burnt his ass a little much with that nugget comment? Don't worry, Burns, we're going to get you to whip those little droopies out soon."

Peter Becks, the machining technician, stepped into the lounge room dressed in his blue jumpsuit with his shaggy hair tied back. "What are you guys doing? Playing poker?" He stuck his empty cup into the water machine and waited while it filled.

"You snap your fingers and say 'titties', and this son of a bitch shows up every time." DalBon thumbed at Becks. "Come get a seat, Becks, we're going to try and get a good look at Reeves's dick here. It's strip poker."

Burns shuffled the cards and dealt them.

"Little too cold for that shit. My nipples can already cut glass." Becks shook his head. "Besides, I suck at poker. Y'all assholes here would have me bareass in no time." He took his cup from the water machine and sipped a drink.

"That a bad thing?" Stalls raised an eyebrow as she picked up her cards. "Come sit your ass down. I want a look at those perky nipples."

Burns shook his head. "Already dealt! He has to wait!"

"What a load of shit, Becks," DalBon said as he pulled his cards over and fingered through them. "If I knew I could just sit out and watch everyone else get naked, I'd have done that too."

"Ahh, I've got shit to do anyway." Becks waved them off. "Fucking sensors are dicked up again. This hand-me-down junk is working on my *last* nerve. Tell you what though, Stalls, if you want a peek at my perky nipples, that can be arranged."

"*Shit.*" She grinned. "I was just being nice, buddy."

"Hell with ya," Becks joked and waved his hand at her. "Tell you what though, you talk Moller into a game then you uhh . . ." He made a phone gesture and stuck it up to his ear. "You give me a call. I got a thing for chicks with glasses." He smiled, showing all his teeth.

Stalls rolled her eyes as Becks left. "Moller? *Please*, she's all over Elliot. Two act like everyone doesn't know they're fucking. Not *that* big of a ship."

Alice shared a quick smirk at Tommy.

"Let's see what we got here." DalBon looked at his cards and then eyed Burns. "Oh, brother, I'm about to beat that ass."

Burns refused to look at him, so instead he angrily stared at his own cards.

Tommy pointed at the deck. "Deal the river. Let's get this shit a'rollin'."

Burns set his cards on the table, then peeled off the top few cards and laid them flat. Each card elicited an excited and exaggerated grin from DalBon as he whispered, "*Yes.*"

"Shut up, man," Burns said as he picked his own cards up. "No way you got that good of a hand."

"Oh, boy." DalBon's smile was wide, and he kept nodding his head. "Just you wait."

"Fold." Tommy sighed and set his cards down.

"Yeah, me too." Stalls laid her cards flat and brushed them toward the center.

"I'm in." Alice kept on her best poker face.

"That's what I'm talkin' about." DalBon nodded and looked at Burns. "You're not turning chicken shit on me, are you, boy?"

"In," Burns said as if his honor depended on it.

"You know I'm in." DalBon flipped his cards over and so did Burns. DalBon won. *"Hell ye—"*

Alice flipped her cards over and won, taking the hand.

"Shit!" Burns brushed his cards toward the center.

DalBon narrowed his eyes as if to inspect her cards. "How's this work then? Am I just supposed to show you my titties, and then I can put my shirt back on? Becks was right about it being too damn cold in here."

"Nope, peel'em off, boys." Alice made a *come here* gesture toward the table. The two peeled their shirts off and tossed them aside.

"I'm gonna get you next hand." DalBon grinned wickedly at Burns.

"We got two chicks in strip poker, dude!" Burns shouted. "Why the hell do you keep focusing on me?"

---

TEALSON WALKED the cargo hold and came up alongside Colton Parker, their loadmaster. "How you doing down here, Parker?" Two weeks out of cryo, and he still felt stiff. Maybe he should have listened to the damned A.I. after all.

"Oh, not bad." Parker's voice was deep. "Not much to do with all this cargo going on hold till we're finished." He stopped to scratch under his chin. "They're not going to make us do the run after Mars, are they?"

Tealson raised his eyebrows and shook his head. "Your guess is as good as mine. Wouldn't surprise me in the least if someone in record-keeping lost track of this cargo all together and they had us floating out here for a month figuring out what to do with it. You know how the Corps is."

"*Orbital Corps*," Parker huffed. "Didn't know I'd be shipping my ass back and forth to Mars when I signed up for the Corps. *Orbital* my ass."

"Name needs an update, don't it?" Tealson agreed.

Barry Smith, the booster engineer, came walking over, his boots clicking on the metal grating of the cargo bay. He had blonde hair and tattoos that climbed up his neck. "That's what you get when you make a whole new branch of the military just because some stupid ass Russkies shoot down a space shuttle on accident."

"Accident?" Tealson frowned. "You believe that shit? I'm sure the goddamn Russians shot it on purpose."

Hands in his pockets, Smith shrugged his shoulders, clearly not giving a damn either way. "Maybe. We might not be a corps for very long anyway. Things are heating up in South America with those Venezuelan rebels, and the word is that the Comanche got ahold of nerve gas again. Cold War's going to turn hot, and they'll need to redirect funds into some other branch of the military.

Tealson tried his hardest not to roll his eyes, but even as he spoke, he wasn't sure if he had succeeded or not. "Cold War has been cold for more than seventy years. Don't expect it to heat up any time soon."

"Don't matter, just saying. All that time and tax dollars thinking the new battlefield was going to be space only to have the Russkies say, 'You know what? You win.' and drop another trillion dollars on Middle East insurgents." Smith grinned, showing his bad teeth. "Just seems a little silly to have the government out here running all this shit when the space race is long dead. Privatize this motherfucker is all I'm sayin'. Then you can start—"

"Yeah, yeah." Tealson waved him off, eliciting a look of irritation from Smith. Tealson had heard it all before. Always from some other grease monkey who thought they could run the country better than the government. "How'd the test on the boosters go?"

"Right as rain," Smith said. "Might need a little kick in the ass as we slow down heading into Mars' atmosphere, but they'll run okay."

"See, saying 'need a little kick in the ass' sounds a little more concerning than you probably meant it." Tealson narrowed his eyes.

"What I'm saying is they passed the test, but you know how this shit works. That is to say, barely."

Tealson still frowned.

"Well, shit. When the time comes, I'll come down here and bang on it with a hammer if need be."

"That makes me feel better." Tealson turned to look at Parker. "That make you feel better?"

"Ehh, boosters and engines ain't my thing." Parker shook his head.

"Yeah, 'bout that . . ." Tealson looked over Smith and then back to Parker. "Your manifest say we got any cigs in the cargo by any chance?"

---

"You got this, boy. I'm team Burns now," DalBon said as Burns picked his cards up. DalBon was already sitting on the cold metal chair stripped down to his underwear. "All that shit-talking I was doing before? It's done. You saying you're going to shave your dick with my razor—"

"He said his balls, not his dick," Tommy cut in. He was leaning back on his chair, also in his underwear.

DalBon held a knowing hand up to Tommy and shook his head. "Water under the bridge, man. I'll even hook you up with my own ball razor. Course, mine has to be about four inches wide for efficiency, so that'll probably take you some time to get—"

"*Shut up*," Burns said flatly to DalBon, staring at him with cold eyes. "My God, do you ever stop running your mouth?" He looked down to inspect his cards again, idly rubbing his tongue against the edge of his teeth in likely the most stressful moment of his life. Alice and Stalls were still in the game and down to their sport bras and panties. It was up to Burns to bring it home, and he still had his pants on.

"Play it cool, kid, and we come out for the win either way here."

DalBon kept talking, sounding like a boxing coach giving a pep talk to his prizefighter. "Winters wins the hand, and Stalls goes topless. Stalls wins, and Winters goes topless. You win, and they both go topless. You can pull this one off. I'm counting on you."

"We're literally sitting right here," Stalls said, shaking her head.

Tommy grinned. "Give the kid a moment, DalBon. He's about to have a damn heart attack."

Alice knew she had them both, though. She had two pairs with the river, and Burns was sweating bullets.

"I'm in," Burns said and nodded his head.

"Throw that shit down then!" DalBon sarcastically bobbed his head.

"Twos and fours," Alice said as she flattened her cards down. "Let me see those panties, Burns."

"Shit!" Burns hissed and tossed his cards onto the table, not bothering to even show them.

"Wait a minute there, sweetness." Stalls chewed a stick of gum and wagged an eyebrow at Alice. "Three of a kind." She laid her cards down. "Let's get a peek at the goods."

"Dammit!" Alice slapped the table and laughed. Burns squeezed a triumphant fist in front of him. "So what? I take off a sock now?" Alice asked.

"We agreed! Socks don't count!" Burns panicked.

Burns's comm, sitting on the table, came alive with Tealson's voice. "Burns, you there?"

He hesitated before he picked it up. "Yeah?"

"Pax says the toilet is backed up again. Go figure it out." Tealson's words were like ice, freezing Burns in place.

"Sir, I'm. . . I'm kind of busy at th—"

"Yeah, I get it, go fix the toilet though. Last thing we need is an overflow. Get on it, kid."

"You heard him, Burns." Stalls thumbed to the hallway. "Go fix the toilet."

Burns shook his head in frustration and stood up, snatching his shirt from the back of his chair. He moped as he walked away.

"Hey, Burns?" Alice called, and he turned around. She raised her bra and flashed the room. Burns's eyes lit up. "That's the last game of poker for me, sweetie, so enjoy it."

DalBon and Tommy laughed their asses off as Burns grinned.

## 4

TOMMY REEVES GROANED and rubbed a hand through his hair as he scrolled across his screen reading the electrical layouts of the station. He was doing his best to prepare for the upcoming job. He had everything he needed, but his head wasn't in it, not fully.

He was thinking about what Alice had told him after the poker game when they were back in his room.

"I'm sorry about before," she had said. He'd only known her for a few short weeks, but they'd spent a lot of time together since then. That was the first time he'd seen her angry.

"Don't worry about it," he'd told her. "Not a big deal. You don't have to tell me everything."

"But I kind of want to. I like you, and I just. . ." She'd seemed pained and conflicted. "I hope this is more than just a *thing* between us."

"Hey, here I was being the one worried about what would happen if they made me move rooms and I lost the bathroom."

She had smiled then, showing her teeth. Her pretty blonde hair tickled her shoulders. She had beautiful hair. "You know John Winters?" the question seemed to come out of nowhere.

The name hadn't rung a bell, though it should have. You can hear names like that all day but the moment someone says them you can't put a face to them because you're not expecting *that person.*

"The senator. He's my father."

John Winters. A power player in the U.S. Senate. Sat on the U.S intelligence committee. Oh yes, Tommy knew him. Senator Winters was on TV every day. Sometimes for bucking the party line, sometimes for a speech on foreign relations. Everyone knew who he was.

"What's wrong?" Yui Tanaka, the ship's information systems technician asked, snapping Tommy from his memories. She'd been sitting behind him, typing away, but he'd all but gotten lost in his own world.

He took a second to compose himself. "Just looking over these schematics again. Can you give me the plans for the sublevel?"

"Of course," she said as her eyes focused on her screen. "What quadrant?"

Alice had also told him that she had been in the Navy and worked with the Marine Corps as a medic.

"I did it as a big *fuck you* to my dad," she'd said, sitting on his bed, her face tight with the pain of the recalled memory. "He kept pushing and pushing for me to go into the medical field. He already had my universities picked out. Had plans of where I was going to do my residency. Everything." A single tear had raced down her cheek then, but her voice didn't so much as fluctuate. "I just want to have a *little* control in my life. A little bit of choice. We argued about it, and I knew how I could get him. *Really* get him. If I enlisted." She'd turned to look at Tommy then, her eyes reddening. "So I did."

He'd put his arm around her, unsure of what else to do, and then things came spilling out.

"They sent me to Libya." Her eyes had been distant, and a coldness had crept into her voice. "I was in Tripoli when Jaysh Alshaeb took it."

*Fuck me.*

Tommy had only thought it, but not said it. The fall of Tripoli had been horrible. He'd seen the pictures of the heads in the streets. American soldiers. A video had made its way around the internet of a member of Jaysh Alshaeb, a celebratory grin on his face as he held up a bag of ears. The man spoke in a foreign tongue, clearly proud of his trophies.

"It got to be. . . too much for me." Defeated, her voice had been flat and stiff. "I got my dad to pull strings. He got me transferred into Orbital Corps."

"Sir?" Tanaka said, snapping him from his thoughts a second time. "What quadrant?"

"Send them all." He slurped some of his coffee. "I've got nothing better to do today."

"What's got you so upset?" The keys clicked beneath her fingers as she quickly brought up commands and had them sent to Tommy. "I thought you were excited to go to Mars?"

He decided to focus on the task at hand. "Yeah, you know, I am. But the more I think about it . . . we don't even know what's wrong over there. We could get there only to find out we need to make a trip back to Earth to get what they need. Long way to go for a game of telephone."

"I hope not. It'd be nice to be home for my son's graduation." Tanaka stared out the window longingly.

"Graduation?" Tommy's brow furrowed and looked back at her. There was no way she was much older than thirty. "What kind of graduation?"

"Kindergarten."

It made Tommy laugh, and he was glad for the humor. "They do that kind of thing for kids nowadays, or is it just a Japanese thing?"

"My sister-in-law is married to an American. Their son had one a year back."

"Well, I hope we make it back for your son's graduation. I'm sure it would mean a lot to him to have you there."

"Oh, he's excited I'm going to Mars. I promised him a Mars rock if I can get one from the station."

"Sounds like a sweet kid." Tommy grinned. "You got a picture?"

"I do." Tanaka's face brightened as she pulled a picture off her console and showed it to him. "This was from just before I left." The picture was of her, her husband, and her son. All dressed formally, but smiling for the picture.

Tommy took the picture for a moment, then handed it back. "Good looking family. Can tell your son is going to be smart."

"Thank you." She put the picture back into place and refocused on her screen. "Would you like me to bring up their last equipment request logs? Might help give you an idea of what could have broken."

He snapped his fingers. "Great idea, toss them my way."

Tanaka nodded and began sorting the logs.

---

TEALSON ITCHED. He'd rationed that pack of candy cane cigs for as long as he could before they were gone, and he was craving even *their* nasty-ass nicotine. Parker hadn't come through for him on finding any in cargo, so now all he could do was sit, wait, and be pissy.

*I'd kill for a cigarette.*

"You gotta be shitting me." Bennie looked over at Tealson from the navigator's booth. "Report is the goddamn Russians are opening talks with the Chinese again. That's all we need, am I right?"

*And I'd start with Bennie.*

They still had a few days to go before they finally touched down on Mars though, and he hoped to God someone had some nicotine to spare down there.

Ignoring Bennie, who spent more time reading bullshit news than navigating, he clicked the comm on the bridge. "You get those sensors working again?"

Becks responded through the comm, *"Ain't shit broken, sir. Just give it a whole reboot and scan again."*

Tealson nodded over to Jeff Regal, the sensor calibrator. "Run the reboot."

"I did," Regal said flatly. "Twice."

"What makes you think it's broken then?" Tealson asked.

"Because it's barely reading anything from their base. Almost no activity. There are a hundred and fifty people on Felicity. This close to the base and those scans should be practically buzzing."

Tealson looked out the window and into the void, considering. "Maybe things are worse than we thought."

Regal grimly shook his head. "What if life support went down with the power? Emergency systems not operating?"

*Then they'd all be long dead.*

Tealson couldn't find a reason to respond to that, so he didn't.

Bennie leaned forward in his chair. "Not necessarily. Maybe they've got a gas leak and they're all in cryo."

"Textbook," Stalls agreed. "System failure means everyone goes into cryo until a recovery team arrives."

"Hundred and fifty cryo beds?" Regal raised his eyebrows. "No way in hell. They've probably got ten or twenty, maybe even the second-gen model that makes your hair fall out if you stay in too long. I bet it's something serious. I bet—"

"That we're about to go shake hands with a bunch of goddamn corpses?" Tealson hissed. "Don't sound so excited about it."

"That's. . ." Regal shook his head. "That's not what I mean—"

Tealson ignored him as he leaned over and hit a new comms button. "Parker?"

A moment later, a deep voice responded. *"Yeah, boss?"*

"Going to need you to prep our atmosphere suits. Looks like Felicity might be in worse shape than we thought. We'll need them prepped in about sixty hours."

*"Got it."* The comm chirped as Parker closed the communication.

"Well." Tealson glanced around at the others on the deck. "Might be a little harder than we anticipated."

---

ALICE STRETCHED as she looked at the monitor. She was running a few medical tests for Lacey Moller, the ship's communications specialist.

Fresh from college and slouching even as she walked, Moller was perpetually nervous and shy. Today, in the examination, was the longest they had ever talked.

"I—" Moller had said as she sat on the medical table wearing nothing but a thin robe that was tied in the back, purposefully avoiding eye contact. "I missed my period."

Alice had nodded, acting as if she wasn't fully aware Moller and Elliot were sleeping together. Orbital Corps had strict policies against crew members sleeping together, but it wasn't uncommon for it to happen on these long trips. Alice could only imagine at least a *few* people knew she and Tommy were together. Moller might be a little different. Awkward as she was, she seemed to think the walls were *soundproof* by the noises she made. Alice had even remarked to Tommy once, "At least she's enjoying herself."

"Elliot and I. . ." She'd looked down when she confessed it.

Of course, Alice had told her the obvious—pregnancy during or after cryosleep was nearly impossible.

That hadn't relieved poor Moller, though, so Alice agreed to run tests. They all came out as she had suspected.

"Well, I've got good news, Moller," Alice said as she walked over to the examination table. "You're not pregnant."

Visibly relieved, Moller exhaled. "What about my period, then? I should have had it a week ago."

"You just came out of extended cryo." Alice's voice was as sweet and understanding as she could make it. "It affects everyone a little differently. It's hard for our bodies to go into that suspended animation state, but don't worry. There aren't any long-term effects. I'm sure, when you're back on Earth your body will return to normal."

Moller nodded, but she chewed her lip nervously, still avoiding eye contact.

"That all? Something else on your mind?" She reached out and patted Moller's hand, half expecting her to recoil from it, but was shocked when Moller gripped her hand instead.

"I've never done anything like this." She looked up at Alice, looking fragile. "I don't know how you do it."

Alice held her hand, nodding and listening. "Is this your first time in space?"

She nodded. "Yeah. First time for a *lot of things.*"

Alice grinned, showing her teeth. "And you're nervous? That's to be expected. It takes a little getting used to, sleeping strapped down in case artificial gravity fails, eating everything out of a plastic tube or silver bag. I promise, it gets easier."

"It's not just that. I don't know how you walk around like that." Moller flicked her eyes toward Alice and then looked away. "I don't know how you do it. You're so confident. . . I don't know what I'm doing. I've never even had a boyfriend."

Alice wasn't sure what Moller meant, but she leaned down to take a seat next to her, still squeezing her hand. "How old are you, Moller?"

"Twenty-one." She looked at Alice, her eyebrows arched up, shy and uncertain.

"Twenty-one, but you've already finished your graduate degree and joined the military. I don't know how *you* do it. So, what is it? You just feel unsure? Don't know what you're doing?" Alice leaned closer, grinning. "No one knows what the hell they're doing at that age, but I've never met a twenty-one-year-old who was where you are. You should be proud, really."

Moller nodded politely, but she didn't look too relieved.

"How did you even get this position, Moller? You're pretty young to be a communications specialist for a cargo team."

"I had. . . good scores," Moller said, but Alice felt like she was underplaying herself. "I heard that things out here are less, uhh, complicated? You just focus on your job, and people don't bother you too much. You don't have people calling you for birthday parties or asking you to go out drinking."

"Yeah, they aren't so strict on regulations. This far into space, and away from command, they don't bother you about haircuts and folded sheets so long as you do your job. But you get crammed in with a lot of men, and they don't all wear deodorant." Alice made a face. "And you hear *a lot* of dick jokes."

Moller exhaled, finally showing some relief. "I don't really mind all of that. Besides, I like Elliot. He's nice."

Alice smiled, but internally she thought otherwise.

*I always thought he was a bit of an asshole.*

"With Elliot, though, is it. . ." Alice raised her eyebrows. "Serious?"

"He's nice," Moller repeated in a way that sounded like *'for now'*.

Chuckling, Alice squeezed Moller's hand. "I think you're going to be fun to work with."

Moller looked up at Alice. "My father, he was in Orbital Corps. He said he signed up right after the Russians shot down Apollo Seventeen. Do you know why we built Orbital Corps?"

"Uhh, yeah." Alice had to think for a moment. "The Russians shot down that shuttle, and everyone thought it was the opening volley of a space war."

"Yeah. Nixon created Orbital Corps right after. My father said it was exciting then. That there was all this hope and optimism right alongside the fear. Everyone thought there was going to be this big war out there and it never happened." Moller went quiet.

Alice nodded, she didn't know what else to say. She'd heard it all before. People either said now that the U.S. won the Space War, or that it was the greatest feint the world had ever seen with the Russians getting the U.S. to waste resources while they focused on world-based assets.

"What I'm saying is. . ." She frowned and looked at Alice. "It's so *not exciting* here."

Alice burst out laughing, and the awkwardness made Moller smile too. "Yeah. Burst your bubble, right?" Alice smiled sympathetically. "It's not like how they told you it'd be, right? Unfortunately, that's just the military in general. You know what, though? Do a few years here, get them to pay off your student debt, and have a nice clean record for your resume. Ship on out, that's what most people do. The *smart* people anyway."

"Is that your plan?" Moller said, looking curious.

It was a good question. One to which Alice did not have the perfect answer. Not one she'd be willing to give Moller, anyway.

*No. As soon as I go home, I have to face my father.*

"I might stay a little longer. I don't need anything *exciting*. Easy work, and I can retire early." She shrugged. "Show me something better, and I might consider it."

"I think it's more than that," Moller said, a small smile touching the corners of her mouth. "I think you're genuinely good at what you do here."

*Good at what? Flying through space on cargo runs? We barely even need a medical officer.*

"Thanks," was all she could think to say. "And, hey, you're good at what you do, too. Don't get so down on yourself."

Moller stood and brushed a loose strand of hair behind her ear. "Thanks, Winters. For everything." She walked to the door and turned, placing a hand in the doorway. "And thanks for calming my nerves. Maybe I can finally get some sleep without worrying so much."

"Any time," Alice said, frowning after Moller left the room.

*Poor girl. She hates it out here in space.*

Alice couldn't really blame her. Other than Tommy, she didn't know anyone who loved being out in this cold, vast darkness. It seemed to suck out a piece of your very soul, slowly at first, but the feeling became more pressing over time.

*She just needs to get out and stretch her legs is all. Hell, we all do.*

*Mars Felicity, here we come.*

# 5

---

ALICE HAD ONLY JUST TAKEN her seat in the small cafeteria, a tray of food in front of her, when Tommy took the seat across from her and set down his tray.

"We've got to talk," he said.

His voice had a startling urgency to it. She half-expected to hear he didn't want anything to do with her anymore.

*Should have kept my mouth shut and just enjoyed it while I could.*

"Okay," she said, sticking a bun into her mouth. She wasn't going to get emotional or anything. She'd been through enough of that with other men already. "What is it?"

Tommy looked over her shoulder, making sure no one was close enough to hear. "After you told me about your dad. . ."

*Here we go.*

She nodded and lazily took another bite.

"I just felt the need to tell you a little bit about my own baggage."

"Oh yeah?" Her eyebrows perked up. It was an honest surprise to her. "Sweetheart Tommy Reeves has baggage?"

"Main reason I joined Orbital Corps."

"It's not exactly an original story," she joked, quoting him. That was true, though. From what little she knew, practically everyone on the ship was there because they didn't have a better option.

"I transferred in from the Air Force. Got this gig because I requested it." He shook his head. "Just got divorced last year. I spent the last ten months of our marriage in Iraq. About the same amount the year before that. By the time I got back, we were just different people." Tommy sighed and hung his head, picking absentmindedly at his food. "She was ready to move on."

Alice nodded. It was a familiar story, and she'd heard it before.

Tommy laughed, but there was no joy in it. He looked away from her. "Hell, I'm already lying about it."

"What do you mean?"

"God, I don't know how much of this shit I want to unload on you." Tommy, still painfully grinning, shook his head.

She snorted. "Well, I told you my bullshit, so let's hear it."

"You know how the military works, right? They're always fucking things up."

"You say that to me like I didn't spend the last seven months on a tour extension."

"At some point, my wife got the report that I was KIA'ed." Tommy looked down at his own tray. He'd yet to take a bite. "Hell, they even sent her a folded flag."

Alice's face soured. "Yeah?" It was all she could think to say.

"I called home, telling her I was up for leave, and she was. . ." He looked up at Alice. "She was surprised, to say the least."

"I bet. Must've been horrible for her."

"That was the thing. She told me it had been, but she'd since *moved on*. It all came spilling out of her, and she didn't even mean to say it when she did."

"Say what?"

*"I'm glad you're alive, but it would be easier if you weren't."*

"Oh my God, she said that?"

*"Yeah,"* Tommy said and straightened up. "She started apologizing right away, but you know what? I understood what she was saying. It'd already been a few months. She wasn't a monster. There

just wasn't anything there for us. I didn't *feel* anything for her anymore. Makes sense right? How else does a *few months* slip by without bothering to give your wife a call unless there just isn't anything there"

"That's why you're here in Orbital Corps?"

Tommy nodded and then reached down to pick at his food. "Both parents are in the grave. No brothers or sisters. I don't have any family on Earth, just bullshit. Can't get further away from the earthly bullshit than Orbital Corps, right?"

"Yeah, I guess so."

"Besides." He smiled, trying to lighten the mood. "I always wanted to see the stars."

*"Here we go again,"* Alice teased.

---

"HOW ARE THE SCANS?" Tealson asked. "See any anomalies?"

Regal sighed. "Are you asking me if I see a blown-up Mars base? Answer's no."

"How about leaking air, jackass?" Bennie grunted, crossing his arms.

"Fuck me, you have some high expectations for this bullshit gear." Regal went back to his scans, spending the next few minutes looking them over.

Tealson felt the urge to tell Regal to shove the attitude up his ass, but truthfully, they were all getting on edge. The closer they got, the worse everything appeared.

It hadn't just been that the communications were down. It appeared power on the whole facility was down. It was anyone's guess if even minimal life support was still functional. The whole mission could quickly turn into a corpse retrieval.

"Hmmm." Regal didn't look up from his screen. They all sat in silence, anxiously waiting.

Bennie shot a look of disbelief at Tealson and then at Regal. "You going to cue us in, princess?"

Regal sneered. "Holy shit, you want me to read the whole damn thing at a glance? Want me to tell you your horoscope too?"

"*Regal*," Tealson said in his 'officer's' voice, forcing Regal to snap to attention. "Can the shit. Give me your current best assessment. Is it safe for us to land on that damn thing, or will we blow ourselves up? Will the docking bay doors even read commands?"

The room went silent again waiting for Regal to answer.

"Current assessment is that it looks safe. The docking bays appear to have some functionality, but it's a hard guess to say if they'll be totally operational or not. It's going to be a lot of fun if we just get here to have to turn around."

"Oh, you don't believe that, do you?" Tealson frowned. "You know we'd just have to put this ship down on the surface and man a foot team into the base." Tealson looked over to his pilot. "Stalls, you can land this bitch, if need be, right?"

"Yes, sir, I can."

"Even still." Tealson pointed at Regal. "Better hope she doesn't have to."

Regal's gaze darted between them before he nodded and returned to his scans.

Twenty minutes later, they were able to signal the bay doors and get them to open. Tealson saw Regal sigh in relief. He shook his head and then pushed the comms button to tell the landing team to prepare for landing within the hour.

---

ALICE NERVOUSLY FINGERED her medical kit. She'd been trained to perform while in an atmospheric suit, but she was long out of practice.

*That's not it. Something changed between Tommy and me since we talked in the cafeteria.*

There it was. Something had changed between them, but she wasn't sure what yet. It had been just two days, but she could feel it.

They were both busy with last-minute prep, and they hadn't even really seen each other since that talk.

Tommy was a nice guy, sure, but it was hard to say if he wanted more than a fling. It wasn't exactly like either of them had many options. He probably wasn't thinking it was all that serious.

*Was he?*

Hard to say. It was hard to know what any of it meant when either of them could get transferred out on the very next assignment. Why bother—

"*Hey.*" Paxton George—"Pax" to everyone on board— nudged her elbow. "Look at that." He pointed out the window as the Mars base came into view.

"That Felicity?" Alice asked as she leaned closer.

"Yep." Pax grabbed his helmet and locked it into place. A puff of air from micro compressors confirmed it was sealed.

A comms transmission from Tealson came through her earpiece. *"Landing crew assemble on the dock. Stalls is putting us down now. We'll touch down in fifteen."*

Procedure was for the medical officer to accompany any landing crew, so Alice had already made her way to the dock. She looked around but didn't see Tommy. He should be part of the landing crew too.

*He's waiting until the last minute. Just because he told you about his ex doesn't mean you're any more than "convenient". You should know it's not worth getting invested when you're up here.*

She tried to ignore the thought, but her mind liked to torture her.

*This is just fun. Why do you have to make it something it's not? Just have fun and don't get wrapped up. It's stupid to invest yourself in—*

"Hey, I was looking for you." Tommy patted her on the back.

"You were?" She straightened, trying not to seem so surprised. "Sorry, just thought we'd meet here."

"No worries. Glad I could catch this, though." He put his elbow against the wall and leaned forward to the glass, watching them descend onto Felicity.

Alice couldn't see his eyes, but she knew the way he was looking at

Mars. That cheesy grin on his face, the anticipation—it made her smile.

---

INSIDE THE PERIHELION'S docking cabin, Alice looked out the window. Felicity's bay doors closed behind them with a mechanical whine. Stalls had put them down inside the station perfectly, and now Felicity was waking up, and like a yawn, the bay's lights flickered with life.

The words *Please Wait* was written in faded yellow paint on the wall, and a red, blinking light just below it blinked, counting down the moments until the bay had fully pressurized.

"Goddamn," Elliot huffed, his voice buzzing from his helmet speaker. "Janky shit. Why's it take so long to pressurize?"

"It was built in the eighties," Tommy responded. "What do you expect?"

Pax flashed a grin back to them. "Just cool your heels until the Commander gives us clearance." His shoulders shuddered. "I'm getting that *roller-coaster-climbing-uphill* feeling right now."

The red light clicked off, and a green light below it blinked on with the word *Cleared* illuminated inside the light.

*"Landing team is confirmed for a go,"* Tealson said over the ship's internal comms. *"Go in and take a peek for us. Keep your helmets on though, until we can get a clear read on minimal life support standards."*

Pax pushed a response button on his helmet and said, "Roger that." The ship's doors opened and he took the first step onto Felicity. He clicked on a light embedded in his helmet. "Low visibility. Turn on your lamp-lights." Pax panned his light around the room. "Last time I was here, they had someone to greet us."

"I think they forgot the red carpet this time," Elliot quipped.

The empty bay sent a chill up Alice's back. An odd sensation of being unwelcomed rolled over her body, as if she was trespassing on someone else's property.

The hangar bay was nearly empty except for supplies. There was no other ship, only a few manned rovers for traversing the surface. After the Russians gave up on the space race, money stopped flowing into Felicity, and it had begun to hollow out. It showed.

Alice looked across the stacks of unwrapped cargo and abandoned supplies. She pointed at one large container and said, "That says rations. They left their supplies here. Whatever happened, happened fast."

"Yeah," Tommy said. "What the hell could make them do that?"

Elliot chuckled nervously. "Maybe some viral STD? You hear about all the fucking they do on stations like—"

Pax cut in, "Hell, Elliot. Cut the shit."

"You really need all this shit?" Tyler Bartlet, the security officer, grunted as he stepped off the ship and set the equipment case down.

"Yeah, you need a hand?" Pax asked him, turning back.

"I'm fine, just hate moving in these damn suits," Bartlet complained as he adjusted the suit around his neck.

They went inside, making their way up to the processing room. The exterior doors were large enough to drive a forklift through, but they were wide open at the moment. Alice noted that was a safety hazard, they were either too lax on Felicity, or it was further proof that everything had happened too quickly—whatever it was. The whole group felt it, and they were silent as they entered the room, only the wheeze and click of their air tanks broke the silence.

Elliot stepped up close to the processing agent's room and looked through the window. The door was closed, but there was no one inside. He cleared his throat. "You think they're all asleep?" Elliot asked, his voice buzzing over the comms. "How many cryo beds does this place even have?"

"Hard to guess. They moved a lot of blacklisted things in and out of here." Tommy answered, following behind. "Not a hundred and fifty beds, though, I'd guess. I'm not even sure where they're at. The schematics are old. They refitted the base with better beds a decade or so back, but they didn't detail where they placed them."

"Well, ain't that goddamned lovely?" Elliot asked. "Doesn't sound like the U.S. government at all to be confused and unorganized."

Alice froze in place, as her thoughts started to shift. The station had a hundred and fifty souls, but it was silent. Such places had a unique *silence*, and it was unnatural. She remembered this kind of silence. She saw it in Tripoli as the locals cleared out.

It meant that something bad was about to happen.

"Hey." Tommy rubbed the back of her shoulder. He said nothing else but raised his eyebrows at her sympathetically.

Smiling politely, she nodded and kept forward.

Tommy moved up to the bay exit—a solid white door that could split down the middle and slide into the walls. It had a small window in it.

Tommy commanded the door to open. "Access." Nothing happened. "Door access." The door stayed still.

Elliot came up and jokingly kicked it. "Open, you bastard."

"Power must be really low if they even diverted door access. No biometrics scans." Tommy opened up a panel, and grabbed the release handle. "Want me to pop the cork?"

"Yeah, let's get inside," Pax said and nodded beneath his helmet.

Tommy twisted the handle and pulled it straight out. Air popped and shot from the door compressors and the doors slowly opened. Brackish water poured in from an apparent flood on the other side.

"Shit!" Tommy said, looking down at the flowing water, which rose to about shin height. "Whole damn place is flooded; that's not good."

"Oh yeah?" Bartlet said, doing little to hide his irritation. "What gives you that inclination?"

"I'm serious." Tommy looked back at him, his light hitting them and casting a shadow back. "You don't get how *not good* it is for this much water to be here. It's not something we can fix."

Pax scanned his light across the area and spoke. "How the hell did there get to be so much of it? Seems like a hell of a lot."

"Well, you need a hell of a lot of water to run a base like that," Tommy said. "Who knows what the hell happened? Maybe the heating quit so a few pipes burst and this is all they've got. *Shit*, this is going to take some major cleanup."

Pax pushed the button for his comms. "You hear that, Tealson? Broken beyond our ability to repair."

"*I heard it,*" Tealson responded across the comms. "*I'll have a message sent to Earth soon. As of now, mission priority has changed. We're here for personnel rescue and to minimize future loss. See if you can determine what happened so I have something to put in my report.*"

"Lovely." Pax scanned his light inside, stepping into the water. Emergency lights spun at the center of the curved ceiling of the hallways. "You think this whole place decompressed?"

"No," Elliot answered, looking at a large, wrist-mounted tool. "Oxygen levels aren't good, but they're breathable. Probably leaking, but it didn't decompress."

Pax nodded and stepped inside. He shined his helmet light down two dark hallways and shrugged. "All clear so far."

Alice followed the rest of the team inside. "What do you think now, Reeves?" she said to Tommy, using the formality. "Top of the line, right? Best the 1980s had to offer."

Tommy looked down one hallway and then another. "Getting me a little freaked out, if I'm being honest."

"Me too," Alice said, feeling her skin prickle as she looked down empty hallways. "Cryos might be in the medical bay. It's probably one of the most secure places on the station. Has to be in case there's some kind of viral breakout."

"It's up here." Tommy panned his light down a hallway as they walked.

"You sure?" Pax asked.

"Positive. I've etched the schematics into my brain."

Treading through water, they headed toward a sealed hallway door. It didn't automatically open as they approached.

Pax gestured at the door. "Pop the cork for us again, Reeves."

Tommy nodded and came up, pulling off the panel and yanking the handle again. The compressors popped, shooting out air, and the door opened.

"*Elliot,*" Tealson's voice buzzed across comms again. "*How are the oxygen levels in there? Same?*"

Elliot looked at his equipment, his gloved hand clicking through screens. "Even worse, but still breathable. Going to leave a taste like old socks in your mouth, though. I doubt the recycling filters are functioning. Nice yellow coating for your throat if you want to try it out."

"Yeah, no thanks," Alice said.

"Lab is up here." Tommy pointed to another sealed room. The door was twice as large as the hallway doors. He stepped up and looked through the window, his helmet light shining inside. "Shit! There's a body in there!"

"Let me see." Alice moved closer and peeked in, her head lamp illuminating the room. Inside the lab, a woman was strapped down to a bed. Her body appeared to be covered by strange growths, finger-sized blisters, but Alice couldn't tell for sure.

The group waited as Tommy popped the handle. The door slowly slid open. Water immediately flooded in, but Tommy and Bartlet were able to snap the doors shut again.

Alice stepped in deeper, scanning her head lamp across the room. The lab was pitch black and much of the equipment had been knocked over. Medical supplies spilled across the floor. "Something bad happened here. Keep your damn helmets on. There might have been a contagion released."

"It's a woman. Fuck me, what the hell is wrong with her?" Elliot was already close to the body, looking it over. "Looks like a six-foot leech is sucking her arm."

Alice could see it now. It had been hard in the darkness and the flashing emergency light. Long, black tendrils hung loosely from her body. The flesh at the base of them was pink and diseased.

"Stay back. Don't touch it!" Alice came closer, shining her light across the body. Her clothes were ragged and torn, a lab outfit. A name tag said Lyndsay Waters.

*God, Lyndsay. I hope you didn't suffer long.*

"*Report,*" Tealson's voice buzzed in. "*What are you seeing there?*"

Pax responded, "There's a woman, she's—"

Lyndsay's hand began to flex open and close.

"Shit!" Alice said, turning to look back at the others, her entire body pimpling in gooseflesh. "She's alive!" She tried not to let her voice shake too much.

"What the fuck!" someone yelled.

"*Report!*" Tealson screamed over the comms.

Alice turned, and the long, leather-like ropes began to spasm and curl in and out. Lyndsay's eyes opened, and they seemed to be coated in a yellow mucus.

"Uhhh," she moaned. Blood leaked from her mouth as her eyes rolled in her head. She weakly pushed against her restraints.

"Bartlet, give me the tranq pen! I don't have one in my kit." Alice called without turning back.

"The fucking—"

"The tranq pen!" Alice screamed "Give me the goddamn tranq pen!"

The tentacles curled and wiggled like worms with rolls of excess skin knotting and unknotting on each end, the sound of it nearly making Alice sick.

"Not getting anywhere near—" Bartlet said as Alice turned and pushed him back from the heavy case.

She pried it open and dug a case with a red medical marker on it. She popped the latches on it and dug out the tranq pen. Her training kicked in, and Alice's hands were calm and steady.

As she turned to Lyndsay, her blood ran cold in her veins. The woman was snarling, and a few of her teeth rolled from her mouth. Alice froze in place—a moment's hesitation in which a thousand thoughts berated her subconsciousness—before the mechanics of training moved her forward. She slammed the needle and pen down into Lyndsay's ribs, feeling it cut through the muscle as a tentacle slowly wrapped around her boot.

"*Tranck,*" Lyndsay's jaw went loose as she hissed out a mocking attempt at words. "*Peyn.*"

Alice's eyes flared open, afraid to look away. "Another one, give me another one!" She felt the tentacle wrap tightly around her ankle but tried to ignore it.

*"Someone answer me, goddammit!"* Tealson screamed over the comm.

*"Give."* Lyndsay's head twisted to look at Alice. *"Me."* Her arm tightened against the restraints and her fingers twisted into claws. *"Another."*

"Get the fuck out of the way!" Tommy shoved Bartlet aside and grabbed another pen, handing it to Alice.

Alice hammered it down, feeling it pierce through breast bone and tissue, and she thumbed down the plunger, injecting the contents into the woman.

Lyndsay's fingers relaxed. The tentacle loosened around Alice's ankles, flopping like a dead fish until it slowed to a twitch. Its fat, wet skin made a strange *pat-pat-pat* sound against the floor.

*"Oh God. . ."* Alice felt her legs start to shake. She backed up, squeezing her hands in front of her. Tommy hugged her, but kept an eye on the collapsed woman.

"W—what the hell *is* that?" Elliot pointed, his finger shaking. "What happened to her?"

*"Report!"* Tealson screamed again.

"Sir," Pax responded again, his voice shaking. "There was a woman. . . Something is—*fuck me*—something is wrong with her. She's sedated now."

"Bring her on board," Tealson said. "Our medical bay has full power."

*"No,"* Alice said, trying to fight back the fear. "Something happened to her. It could be contagious. We need to seal this off. No personnel without suits."

"She's right, Commander," Tommy said. "We need someone to close those dock doors too."

There were a few moments of silence from Tealson, and then: *"Affirmative. I'll send a team. Full decontamination procedures upon return."*

"I'm going to look her over," Alice said, staring at the woman in both fear and curiosity. "We need to know what happened."

*"Affirmative,"* Tealson responded again. *"Bartlet, set up auxiliary power to the lab."*

"Shit," Tommy hissed. "Just be careful."

The others kept talking behind her, but Alice could barely hear them. She was too drawn in. She knew they were going to have to strap down those tentacles too, but that wasn't what was on her mind at the moment.

Instead she was thinking about Lyndsay, and how long she'd been trapped here, left alone in the dark...

*How did she survive here so long without food and water, and where the hell is everyone else?*

# 6

Deep within the cold husk of the Felicity base, the cryo beds still hummed with life. Encased in one such bed was Will Braun. Cryo had frozen him in suspended animation, but his mind still worked...

It still dreamed.

In that long-ago dream, Braun stood idly by, watching through a dirty window as crowds of men and women formed on the sides of the muddy dirt road. Fear held them in place as the soldiers marched past, their boots stepping in unison.

Women wailed, and some reached out, their husbands holding them back with pained expressions on their faces.

Braun sipped his coffee.

Men were pressed up against a wall, and, though Braun couldn't hear them from his perch behind glass, he could imagine what they were saying as the firing squad lined them up.

Braun took another drink.

A man entered the room behind him and gave the standard greeting. Braun turned to him and asked, "What is it?"

"I was told to notify you. They will be venting today. You should expect offensive odors. Perhaps worse than before."

Braun nodded. "And the staffing?" He motioned toward the firing squad. "This unpleasant business hasn't hurt our labor too much, has it?"

The man began to quake then and fade back into Braun's memory. The powerful smell that lived with Braun even to today was upon him. Still vivid. Still real and penetrating.

He felt stuck in place, in time. Trapped by his own anxiety, an invisible hand held him in position. The smell of burning flesh filled his nostrils. He tried in vain to snap out of it.

*This isn't really happening, not anymore. You're not in the motherland Braun. Just wake up. Wake. Up.*

If only it was that easy. Cryo tended to affect everyone differently, and Braun had always been especially susceptible to dreams—nightmares, if he was honest with himself—and this level of cognitive awareness could only mean one thing.

*I'm coming out of it.*

Something different came to him now, and he was at the window once more, watching as he had before. This time, though, he felt something slink into the room behind him as he watched the mindless, uniformed agents of terror passing by in the street. A slave to his memories, he sipped his coffee, though truly what he wanted was to turn or run.

Instead, he watched from the window and took another sip, a slave to memory and a different time—to the ambitions of another man.

The dreadful creature—its breathing uneven and hoarse—paralyzed him with fear. It wasn't the man from before. He knew this instinctively. He felt its jagged, abrupt movements behind him as it came closer. He took a deep breath as a dark, shadowy hand gripped his shoulder.

He let out a scream, liquid bursting from his lungs. His eyes opened, looking through a haze of cryo soup. In the vagueness of the cryo bed, he saw his door rising. He stuck his fingers up and felt cold air. Gripping the sides of the bed with shaky and unsteady hands, he pulled himself up, his back and legs refusing to function initially. As his mouth broke the surface, he gulped in air and found the strength to hang his head over the edge. Gagging, he purged the cryo substance that acted just as the fluid in a mother's womb.

Shivering and naked, his legs slowly warmed and became functional. He slid out one arm and then got a heel over the lip of the bed. The liquid dripped off him, slapping to the floor with loud *plops*. He looked across the room, still hazy, and wiped the thick gel from his eyes, which buzzed and clicked as they focused.

The cryo beds were of an older generation and far more torturous to endure. Temporary amnesia was par for the course, and Braun found himself susceptible to it.

*Why was I in cryo?*

To that, he had no answer yet, but he was calm and knew he would soon understand.

Shaking uncontrollably, but with no desire to stay in the cryo bed any longer, he dug himself out and put his feet to the floor. The bitter cold of the metal and non-functioning heat system was more painful than when he had the mechanical eyes embedded into his skull.

But he was such a man that pain did not deter him. He understood that it was not a real thing, but only a function of the mind, and this was a simple one.

*This place is cold, and you will die if you remain naked.*

As he stepped away, his bed's door began to descend automatically, and a feminine voice from the computer spoke. *"After extended cryosleep, two hours of daily exercise is recommended to avoid injury."*

Looking to his side, there were rows of cryo beds, nearly all with their doors opening. Other men and women were climbing out too, each naked as if born again and looking at him with fear and confusion plastered on their faces as they purged the thick cryo fluid.

*What happened? Who are these people?*

A rising sense of panic clouded his brain, but he held it at bay. There must be a reason, he was sure, but typically, weren't there operators to aid with awakening from cryo? Shouldn't there be a team on standby with clothing, food, and most importantly, answers? There was a woman out and working at the terminals, but she too was naked and dripping with cryo fluid.

Memory was slow to return, but he quickly understood the situation. Whatever happened had been something terrible.

*We heard a knock.*

Braun blinked, his mechanical eyes buzzing and turning to focus as he looked across the room. He wiped a hand across his face, and shook off the jelly.

*We heard a knock. Something's there.*

"How do you know?" Braun whispered to the memory, still feeling half-mad.

*Because it spoke to us.*

Braun's eyes widened, and he suddenly remembered it all, the crushing wave of memories making him stumble until he caught himself on a table. He lived it all once again.

*We heard a knock,* a smiling lab technician named Mark Rufus had said.

*What's it doing? Is it powering up?*

The gate. They built it.

Something else had turned it on.

*What the hell is that? What's that noise?*

The clicking. The horrible, God-forsaken clicking, as the eyeless creature had put its head through the murky, bleeding tear in reality. The fleshy folds on its face peeling open like rotten fruit to reveal its teeth.

*It's coming through!*

It had come in and grabbed the man closest to it. They'd all been too shocked to do anything but watch as it killed him. Killed wasn't the right word. It had *destroyed him.*

*No. Stop.*

Braun tried to pull the reins of his mind and take control once more.

But his mind was still racing.

In his memory, a woman had fallen to the ground, throwing up. Braun had thought it a violent reaction to seeing a man ripped in half in front of her. But then realization had struck.

She had turned.

Then she had killed.

*Stop! You are in control! You are in control!*

For a man like Braun, nothing was more terrifying than the loss of thought and an inability to think rationally.

Another memory came, again filled with blood and gore, but Braun choked it back. He screamed inside the cryo room as he restrained the flood of memories, knowing, *insisting* upon living in the present moment and slowing his thoughts to a trickle.

He heaved in breath, gagging more cryo soup with each exhale until he was once again himself and once more in control.

*Clear your mind. Consider. Evaluate. Plan.*

*How long has it been?*

The reading on the bed told him. Seven months and three weeks. Seven months and three weeks in the womb of a cryo bed. Seven months and three weeks awaiting rescue.

*Seven months and three weeks of nightmares.*

It didn't matter. He had programmed the unit to awaken him if the docking bay opened, and clearly it did, or he would not be out here now in the cold world.

"We have to get up," Braun said as he straightened his back, feeling weak and exhausted. "The air . . ." He took a deep breath, and it chilled his lungs. "The oxygen is low."

He moved to a terminal and flipped several communication switches, but all they gave were dull clicks.

"They're not working." It was Tonya Foulks, his research assistant. She had made her way out before him and already tried the commands. Her blonde hair was plastered to her head with cryo liquid. She pulled a jacket over her shoulders, shivering. "They shorted out; I already tried."

The remaining crew members were climbing from their cryo beds. Some screamed and panicked, while others looked around in confusion. Not all had such violent reactions as Braun. Cryo affected everyone differently.

"What are we going to do?" a red-haired woman shrilled, cowering to hide her nakedness.

A bald man with tired eyes pointed at the door, his voice wavering as he spoke. "We woke up, so that means someone's here! We set it so it wakes us up if the docking bay doors open. All we have to do is sit and wait. It's probably the military. All we have to do is sit and—"

"Who are you?" a young man, chilled with fear, screamed. "I don't know where I am!"

"Someone get over here and help me," yelled an older man with a thick beard, more annoyed than afraid. "I'm cold!"

Braun silenced the room and held up a hand, still naked and dripping. "Every one of you, stop and listen. Get dressed. Immediately. Your memory will return shortly."

One by one, they complied, and Braun could tell that their memories were slowly returning, as more took to weeping.

Braun gathered his clothes and finished buttoning his collar. The sluggish feeling of cryo was still on him, and his legs felt numb. "We have to leave soon."

"Those things might still be out there," the red-haired woman exclaimed, wide-eyed in a panic. "I'm not leaving."

Tonya got closer to the door and looked out. "The station flooded. It's filled with water."

"What?" Braun hissed and moved closer to the glass for a better view. "Something malfunctioned. . ."

Had it been those things? Had they torn the base apart? Had *they* been the ones to somehow open the docking bay, perhaps even by accident? There were more questions, many more, but there was little time.

But the numbness in his legs. . .

Still at the door, Tonya angled herself to look both ways. "I don't see any of them. I think I can make it to the docking bay." She pushed her slimy hair off her face and straightened her shoulders. "I can get to the front and let them know you're all here. I'll just have to be fast."

He heard Tonya, but he didn't respond. He still felt like he was in a fog, the cogs of his mind were not yet fully turning. He didn't want her to go alone.

It was hard for Braun to put his trust in another.

One of Braun's eyes locked in place, the mechanics failing to focus. *"Dammit,"* he whispered and looked away, rubbing it with the tip of his finger.

"I can make it, Braun. I can get there. I'm fast. No one here is ready to move, not after being in cryo for so long. I'm fine though. I feel good. I'm not foggy. I'm clear and sharp."

Braun's eye spun and clicked, trying to find focus. His body needed time to recover.

She was right.

"Okay," he said, looking up to Tonya, closing the bad eye in favor of the good. "Fast and quick. We don't know what happened to those *things*. We don't know if they starved to death, or if they're going to be waking up. *Just be quick.*"

Determined, she nodded her head. Braun gestured for two men across the room to come help pull the doors open. They came over and worked with him to get them pried as far as needed then let them snap shut again as she slipped out. Braun watched her disappear beneath the flashing emergency lights.

They were few now. Looking across the room, he could see that. Fifteen people had crawled from the cryo beds. Fifteen cold and naked people.

*But there had been twenty.*

Amongst the rows of beds, Braun saw one was closed. The glass shell was cracked in a spider-web pattern. Sucking in a breath through his nose, Braun walked closer. He could see the man inside had been asleep, but the elements had leaked in. He was curled up like a mummy, his lips pulled back from yellowed teeth and his muscles shriveled like dried beef. He'd starved to death without even knowing it. His bony jaw protruded, and somehow his face appeared both apathetic and terrifying. Braun was sure the other four were the same.

He appreciated that there was no smell.

*Unsupervised cryosleep in malfunctioning, outdated machinery. Twenty participating, fifteen surviving. Seventy-five percent survival rate.*

The odds were cutting close, and the attrition rate was not in

Braun's favor, though he was not afraid. Of the hundred and fifty souls manning Felicity, there now remained only fifteen.

Braun would survive, of that he was sure. Fate had plans for men like him. His great mind was not destined to end with such a bad roll of the dice. Death had often been a companion of Braun's, but it was always with others paying the cost. Other souls to feed the void.

"Tonya won't get past them," the red-haired woman said, her voice cold. "There's too many of them."

"You better hope she does," Braun said, and he meant every word. She'd better, because it wouldn't only be Tonya who suffered. "Get ready, because we won't be able to stay here. If Tonya doesn't get to them quickly. . ." Braun looked across the band of cold, dripping survivors, and then out into the darkness behind the glass. ". . . they're going to turn the power on again."

## 7

TOMMY PRESSED the button for his comms. "We got it fully strapped down and tranqed. Winters thinks those. . . tentacles. . . must have grown after they had the woman locked down the first time because they were loose. We've got a battery hooked up now, and she's running scans."

"*Confirmed,*" Tealson replied. "*Can you run diagnostics and see if we can turn the power back on for the whole facility and get everything functional?*"

"Yeah." Tommy swallowed and looked away from Lyndsay. "Shouldn't be too hard."

"*I'm sending Burns in for an extra hand. Take him and Pax with you.*"

"Confirmed. I'll be waiting." Tommy switched the comms off and shook his head.

*This is fucked.*

"Hmm. . ." Alice looked at a screen while a machine scanned a flashing light over the unconscious woman. "This is strange."

"Yeah? Which part?" Elliot narrowed his eyes in mock seriousness. "The tentacles, or the fact that you keep getting close to it?"

"There aren't any lungs," Alice said, matter-of-factly, a hint of fascination in her voice.

"What do you mean?" Tommy asked, glancing back.

Alice looked up from the screen. "I mean they *aren't there*."

Tommy hesitated, swallowing a mouthful of spit. He hit the comms button again. "Commander, did Burns leave yet?"

*"No. He's getting suited up. What is it?"*

Tommy stared at a limp tentacle. The very end of it dangled from the table. It reminded him of the earthworms he used to find writhing on the sidewalk after rain storms when he was a kid.

"Send him with rifles," Tommy said without peeling his gaze away.

*"That bad?"* Tealson replied.

"Never seen anything like it, Commander."

*"Confirmed. But you keep your goddamn safeties on, and use them only if threatened. Last thing we need is one of you plugging a civi."*

"Confirmed." Tommy began to pace the room. Alice continued her study, and he watched her with strange amazement. She was focused and fearless in her curiosity. In a way, it was frightening.

*Like a kid poking a half-dead animal.*

Minutes later, Burns showed up, his face pale and eyes wide. He had four Orbital Corps standard XTU, short barrel automatic rifles slung over his shoulder. "Where is it? I want to see it."

Pax grunted and pointed toward Alice. "Give me that rifle and go take a look, kid. Knock yourself out." Pax took one and checked to see if it was loaded. "I don't even like guns." He chambered a round. "Can't even remember the last time I had one that wasn't in a video game."

Burns kept one and Bartlet and Tommy took the other two. Elliot held out his arms. "What the hell? Shit like this is why I hate you guys."

"What's wrong with her? She sick?" Burns asked, his knuckles tight on the stock of his rifle.

"Yeah, you idiot," Elliot hissed. "She's *really* fucking sick." He pointed at Burns's gun. "Don't you aim that at anyone."

"Shut up, Elliot." Tommy chambered a round in his own rifle. "All right, you two ready? Keep the safeties on." Tommy looked at Pax and Burns. They both nodded, and Tommy looked to Alice. "Be careful, all right?"

"Yeah, you just be fast. Don't take too long," Alice said. She turned and began running scans again.

"Got it," Tommy assured her, his voice wavering only the slightest bit. "And Elliot," he waited for the man to look at him. "Cut the bullshit and just watch Winters' back, okay?"

"Should have brought me a gun too then," Elliot said, his irritation clear. "But fine." He shrugged. "What the hell else am I going to do anyway?"

Alice turned from her work on the creature and nodded at Tommy. "Be careful."

---

"COMMS ARE DOWN, THAT'S ALL," Pax muttered, his voice sarcastically light. "*Beats a cargo run, doesn't it?*" He puffed out air and shook his head. "What a *fucking* joke. Didn't sign up to Orbital Corps to be walking around with a damn rifle in the dark. I don't even like scary video games."

Tommy grunted in agreement. "The sooner we can get the damn lights on, the better."

"How much farther is it?" Burns scanned his head lamp against the walls. "How can you even know where you're going in the dark like this?"

"I read those schematics a hundred times, and the power room is close to the heart of this place. We're almost there."

"Took us twenty minutes to walk this damn far, so I *hope* it's close." Burns complained as he continually scanned across the dark. "Big ass base."

"It might take you two hours to walk the entire station," Tommy said. "*Big* isn't the right word."

"Yet we still haven't seen anyone," Pax said. "You'd think we'd at least see—"

"*They're in cryo.* We know that already," Burns said quickly.

"Sure as hell isn't all of them. We should've seen *something*. Hell, even a body."

"That bitch back in med bay wasn't enough for you?" Burns retorted. "If I was in charge, we'd plug her in the brain and then *go home*."

"Not a bad idea, kid. Maybe we *should* put you in charge," Tommy snorted.

*Hell, like you haven't thought of the idea yourself?*

"What the hell do you think it is, though?" Pax asked as they came to a door. "I've never heard of anything like that before."

"No clue here, buddy." Tommy pulled the panel off and grabbed the handle. He groaned as he yanked it open, popping the door free. He looked back, and Burns had his rifle pointed right in Tommy's direction. "Dammit, aim at the ground!"

"Yeah. . . got it," Burns replied, his eyes wide as saucers. "Sorry."

*The kid's scared shitless.*

Tommy began to wonder why he wasn't.

*Because you've got a problem. You need to get the power back on. Focus on that. Don't think about—*

"I played this video game once. These things would come out of the walls. . ." Pax hesitated to look across the room. "Eyes were yellow, just like hers. Looked like they were rotting. And they had tentacles, but theirs were—"

"Shut up, Pax," Tommy said, scanning the walls now himself. "Focus."

"Hated that game. But just saying. What if there's another one, and it's *not* strapped down?"

"If it comes at you, we're cleared to shoot it," Tommy began, "I don't know what else to—"

"What the hell was that?" Burns asked, the light from his helmet shining down the hallway. He aimed his rifle. "I saw something move down there."

*"No, you didn't,"* Pax hissed, but he aimed his rifle in the same direction. *"You didn't see shit."* He sounded more interested in convincing himself than anyone else.

Tommy froze in place. His breathing stopped as he clutched the rifle. His eyes became deadly focused.

They all waited. Silent and steady.

Nothing came.

"I told you," Pax said. "There wasn't anything. Get it together, Burns."

"It's all right. We're fine." Tommy stepped closer and carefully pushed down the end of Burns's rifle. "Right here's the power room."

There was no door, but a round opening that led into the room. They walked inside onto grating and noticed the water had filled up the lower floor of the power room.

"Shit, what can we do about that? You sure we won't fry this whole place if we flip the switch?" Pax asked. "Electricity and water don't mix so well."

"I'm going to check." Tommy pulled his pack off and set it down. He fished out a smaller computer and connected to the control module to run a diagnostics check. It took a few minutes with lines of code zipping across the screen as it tested vulnerable points. "I think we'll be fine," Tommy said, finally. "It doesn't look like it's going to fry anything."

Pax nodded. "Your call. Fry the grid, and Orbital Corps might take your paycheck for the next thousand years."

Tommy huffed. "Better pass this up the chain then." He pressed a button on his helmet to open a comms channel. "Commander, it looks like I can flip the switch. I don't think it's going to fry anything. They probably turned it off when they went into cryo because of the leak."

There was a brief moment of silence as Tommy waited for a reply. He looked to both Burns and Pax who shrugged. "Commander?" Tommy said into the comms again.

"*Confirmed. I'm just thinking.*" Another long pause. "*Okay, turn it on.*"

"Confirmed." Tommy moved over to the heavy manual switch, hesitated for a moment, glancing to both Burns and Pax, and pulled it up.

# 8

HERS WAS a mind unlike any other—a thousand thoughts at once. A hive of memory and instincts fed into her, for she was the one of no birth. The one of no beginning. She had always existed, and forever would. Before there was light in this world, she lived. Before the ground had formed and things moved upon it, she lived.

Deep within the core, she had slept. A thing of no beginning, and a thing that would have no ending.

Her flesh shriveled and burned in continuous formation and growth. Ever changing. She was something of instinct, with a single purpose to all of her existence.

*Feed.*

When she had awoken, the world had fallen, and all within it were made to serve. The memory of its resistance had long faded, for she had no equal to encounter, no concept of loss or defeat, only the inevitability of her desires and those who would succumb to them.

But as the world was bled dry and all brought into submission, a sensation she had never encountered took hold.

*Hunger.*

With none upon which to feast, hunger boiled within her.

*Starvation.*

Her children willed themselves to her and her great purpose, and she fed upon them. But a time would come when even her children were no more. And what then for her, the one who was endless, when there were no more children to feed upon? When all the world became barren and void?

Ever changing, she took that which the dead had left. Setting her children upon them. Complex artifacts with purposes she did not understand, nor cared to ever attempt. Her children, ever changing and evolving but forever submissive, worked upon the artifacts until a way was made through which her desires could spread.

The artifacts burned with energy and heat so intense, the fabric of reality bled, and new dimensions opened.

Hunger was quickly forgotten and again became a thing unknown to her.

Tireless feeding began as her children took strange shapes and erected new gashes in reality. They set upon the worlds left unknown to her, and tribute was wrought from the inhabitants and brought to her from which she fed.

Screaming, strange things she had never seen, but desired to taste.

Worlds fell as her children ravaged and took from them, all within her name and for her desires.

The beings resisted, but all fell. All would feed her until none remained on this world, this reality, or any other.

When all had come to know her and her hunger, when all—including her children—had fallen to her desires, then she too would be consumed by her hunger.

She was a queen with a throne upon which she still sat. A desire of hunger echoed from her. Her children set out, their one purpose being servitude.

A new world was found, one that did not know of her, but soon would. Things that walked upright and made noise by which to understand one another. The wall had been thick, and her children and their artifacts had not the ability to pierce it. But her children, ever changing and evolving, mimicked the strange sounds of the others, more from a systematic understanding than a true comprehension of thought. The beings complied and built upon their reality such an artifact to pierce the wall.

A gate had been opened, and her children had initiated the tear that caused the hole in reality to bleed.

This bleed was one of many and of no particular importance. Shortly after its opening, it closed, with several of her children already through it.

None of this mattered. None of this was a concern.

Only her desires were of importance. Only her needs.

Only her hunger.

In time the tear would bleed once more. In time she would know that world. She would feed, and she would do so until there was nothing left upon which to consume.

## 9

WILL BRAUN PACED THE ROOM, getting the blood flowing once more in his legs. He listened to the other scientists trying to keep it together— some were handling it better than others. The dried corpses lying in the cryo beds did nothing to help the situation. A few amongst them were crying, some frantically chattered amongst themselves, and others sat off alone in apparent deep contemplation.

"Why haven't we heard back from Tonya yet?" the red-haired woman asked. As Braun's memory cleared he thought she was a member of the astronomy division. "This is what I was telling you. She's not going to—"

The woman continued, but Braun stopped listening. "*Halt deine fresse*," he muttered under his breath.

"To be fair," Leonard chimed in, looking even more bald and ridiculous after the long cryosleep, "we don't know anything about the people who've arrived here. It could be the U.S. military for all we know. We probably don't have anything to worry about. Right?"

Braun sat staring at the same place on the wall, seemingly lost in thought as his mechanical eyes whirred and clicked. He took a deep breath.

*Two hours. Tonya has been gone for two hours. Typical, uninterrupted walk directly to landing bay is approximately thirty or forty minutes. Likely faster for Tonya, who is young.*

*Threats unknown and likely clustered. Ability to bypass easier before they disperse.*

*Two hours, when forty minutes would suffice. Possible reasoning? Forced hiding. Diverted routing.*

*Death.*

*Likelihood of death? Indeterminable with current known factors.*

"Braun!" Leonard snapped. "Are you even listening to us?"

"Don't expect him to answer you," the red-headed woman said, wiping a long strand of hair from her eyes. "He's too good for the rest of us. You can see it on his smug fucking face."

*Fucking Americans.*

A loud hum buzzed from deep down the corridor, and Braun's greatest fear became realized. His eyes grew wide as his hands trembled. The hum of electrical current filled the lightbulbs in the room and the computer stations. Braun flipped a desk over and cursed.

"Scheisse! Gottverdammt!"

*The fools! The goddamn fools!*

Doing very little to hide his fears, Leonard shouted, "The power's back on. They must be pouring through the gate by the dozens!"

Braun ambled over to a console with a vid-screen, his hands trembling slightly as he waited for the boot-up sequence to finish. The room was filled with a cacophony of beeps, hums, and shrieks—both human and otherwise. Finally, the load screen finished, and Braun typed in his credentials and then a series of commands to switch the feed to the gate room.

"*Those fools*," he mumbled to no one in particular. He watched in dread as the gate sizzled and popped, looking like an intensely hot green flame. It was burning a hole from one reality to the other. Hellish creatures came through, strange limbs pulling the creatures along in jerking, unnatural movements. Their heads whipping about looking for meat.

*Hungry. They come through hungry.*

Braun clicked his commands, and the power room came up. It's sublevel had filled with water, but it seemed to be operating. Three men were there, talking and looking over the modules. Whatever they were saying, Braun couldn't understand. He couldn't speak to them or tell them, *Turn it off now!* all he could do was watch.

*They look loud. Quite loud.*

He clicked the commands and cycled through the vid-screens. The first took him to the docking bay, and he inspected the markings on the ship.

"Hmm," he said and pressed the button to change. Room after empty room appeared on the screen until one popped up and the creature was there. The one that had first come through the gate.

The one that ate his colleagues.

It was an interdimensional being. A true curiosity that, under other circumstances, Braun would love to study. But that was not his concern at the moment. He knew where it was heading as it found a deep end of water to submerge itself, and he saw the once-human creatures following in its wake.

*It's heard all the loud noise in the power room.*

"Gott helfe uns allen," Braun whispered in prayer and clicked the cameras off. He had no real interest in watching what came next.

"The gate. . . it's open?" asked a young scientist, the son of the station chief, if Braun was not mistaken. "Braun, what do we do?"

Braun didn't answer him. He was too busy thinking. "*Shh,*" he commanded, holding a finger to his lips.

*Tonya has failed. The gate has opened. Whatever the rescue team is, they will be overrun. Options are diminishing.*

Braun looked across the survivors. Each was assuredly a critical thinker, but handicapped in thought by fear and confusion. Braun had no such afflictions.

"The plan doesn't change. We should just wait," said the red-haired woman. "They're going to come! They're going to rescue us!"

"I think not," Braun said, assured of little, but certain that whatever rescue team arrived, they would not be able to get to them.

"Then what are we supposed to do?" the son of the station chief asked again.

"Gather whatever weapons you can, and prepare yourself." These were not the men and women Braun would have chosen, but they were the ones he had. "We will have to fight our way across the station."

THE LIGHTS FLICKERED and buzzed as they came to life. Computer modules clicked and blinked as they booted up, a series of text scrolling across them.

"We got it," Tommy said, looking over to the others, his face a beacon of contentment. "Shit, we actually did it." He felt as if his nuts were going to crawl inside of his body and never come back down. "Let's see what the flooding is all about."

He headed toward one of the consoles and began typing. A request for credentials came up, and he plugged a USB into a port that gave him emergency administrator access.

He clicked through readings and commands for a few minutes, reading lines of code.

"*Hey,*" Burns said, looking down. "Water is starting to stir?"

Pax looked up. "You get the turbines going, Reeves?"

"No, I haven't turned anything on." Tommy stepped over to the edge of where the water pooled and looked. It was swirling slightly.

"Well, turn them on and see if we can pump this out." Pax pointed back to the console.

"Hell, I don't know." Tommy watched the water for another moment before moving back to the console. "I think we better get

Elliot and Becks to take a look at the readouts before I start flipping switches."

"Fine with me. Let's just get the hell out of here then." Pax smirked in relief.

"Roger that," Burns said, looking the facility over and breathing hard.

Tommy stepped down as Pax hit his helmet comms. "Commander, we—"

A burst of static filled the air, causing Pax to flinch. Tealson spoke on the other end, the transmission coming through broken and jumbled, "*Say again?*"

Pax pushed the button again, trying to speak over the static. "I said we've reconnected the. . ." Pax's words trailed off as he looked down. A long, leech-like tentacle stretched from the sublevel filled with water. It had already come too close, and as Pax pulled away, it snapped up around his ankle and took him off his feet. He huffed as he smacked his back against the floor and the air pushed from his lungs.

Time became strange. Everything happened so fast that Tommy only watched in a strange sense of amazement, but the details burned into his eyes with a memory that would never be forgotten. Pax had barely been able to utter the slightest of screams before he was pulled hip deep into the water.

A pale beast unlike anything Tommy had ever seen rose from the water. Its limbs were long and corded with muscle. It had strange, curling fingers, and joints that protruded from its chest. More limbs rippled from its back and helped to push itself out of the water. Its head was nothing more than a large nub, peeled open like a flower. The slimy, grasping tentacle protruded from a mouth full of teeth.

In no way was this like the woman in the med lab. It had no resemblance to anything human. It had no eyes or cheeks that could express anger or joy. It had only a body seemingly designed to kill.

And it used it to tear Pax apart.

*Help him.*

The thought was quick, sliding up in the front of Tommy's mind, but his body refused to obey. His feet stayed planted to the floor, as if they were made of concrete. His eyes widened in horror, disconnected from all but the barest thought or reason.

Pax's screams rose in intensity as the small, slender joints on the creature's chest uncoiled and grabbed at Pax's torso, pulling it aside and tearing the suit with ease, causing a burst of air.

More things came up from the water, something that looked like a dead man with a broken jaw, his hands completely gone and replaced by thick, wriggling vines. The other was a woman with growths stretching across her mouth and up her head, her skin bloated and her eyes dead, but her hands reaching for the living.

*We have to. . .*

The gears of his mind turned, but his feet stayed planted.

*. . . have to . . .*

Pax shrieked and pushed at them. The inhuman thing's leech dug into his stomach. The human-like things fell upon him and tore his suit off, grabbing at his flesh and biting.

*. . . to . . .*

It plunged what seemed to be its head into Pax's stomach, chewing out his innards as it pulled back. Pax screamed and shot one hand in Burns's direction as he was dragged into the water. Water and blood sprayed onto Burns's suit.

*Run.*

As Tommy sprang forward, Burns too was backpedaling, his own screams of terror rivaling those of Pax's. The man with tentacle hands crawled out of the water, his jaw loose and screaming, and jolted forward with startling speed. He slammed the fat tentacles against Burns's arm and wrapped against it, pulling with such force Burns's glove tore off and the skin became exposed. The woman dove and took a bite from Burns, making him scream in pain.

Fear and panic gave way, and Tommy reacted, not with thought or consideration, but with pure instinct. He lurched forward to grab Burns and slid his arm under Burns's. "Come on!" he screamed, even as they tried to pull Burns down into the water.

The woman's grip was tight, and her jaws worked against Burns's forearm. She huffed in delight as she gnawed, Burns's blood filling her mouth.

"Get off me!" Burns screamed and thrashed, his voice breaking. "Get her the hell off me!"

Tommy groaned as he strained against them, pulling Burns back as the creatures dragged him toward the water.

They were far too strong, too crazed and violent. Tommy's boot slipped as he too was jerked forward.

He was losing, and Burns would soon be dead.

Tommy let go, and Burns instantly slapped to the floor. His eyes were filled with desperation as Tommy pulled his rifle up, firing off a burst of rounds into the creatures' faces and chests. Red roses of blood bloomed and bone splintered as the things released unearthly howls. They recoiled, letting go of Burns.

"Come on, kid!" Tommy yelled as he pulled him to his feet, causing Burns to shout in pain.

"Motherfuckers!" Burns roared, grabbing his own rifle from the ground. He opened fire on the creatures, fresh wounds popping in place as they spasmed from the impact.

More creatures came from the water and the darkness beyond, each unique in its mockery of flesh. Tentacles grew from the back of one woman and lashed the air in continued frenzy. Another was hunched over and naked, its breasts swollen and green while basketball-sized boils jiggled on its back. A third came from the dark, its fingers much larger than any man's and missing half its face.

What remained of Paxton George floated to the surface, just as the creatures crawled from the abyss. He was no longer screaming. They all fell upon him, taking what little remained.

And there was little. Nothing of Paxton George had remained distinguishable to show that he was once a human being with emotions, thoughts, and ambitions. He had been a man who did his job, rarely complained, and when given the choice, enjoyed playing video games in the company of others. He had a girlfriend who sent him transmissions and was currently attending college. She'd asked Pax to join her. If he had seriously considered it, Tommy didn't know.

Now Pax was only meat.

Tommy knew if he and Burns didn't get out of there, they would share the same gruesome fate.

Burns still screamed and fired, but the creatures kept moving, refusing to die.

The inhuman monstrosity that had torn apart Pax emerged from the water, shaking violently as it still held part of him in its mouth. It grabbed another piece and descended into the water once more. With all the meat gone, the things, which were apparently humans at one time, all screamed and came forward for more lively prey.

They wore torn lab coats, ripped overalls, and shredded pants. They were humans once.

People.

*These are the people who lived and worked on Felicity. My God, this is worse than we could've ever imagined.*

Compelled by fear, Tommy unleashed another volley of fire, and again saw how useless it was in slowing their approach.

"My arm!" Burns screamed even as Tommy fired. The bullets shredded their chests, blew off arms, and splattered their heads.

But they kept coming.

A headless creature with only one arm and a tentacle reaching from open wounds on its chest came close before the impact of Tommy's rifle sent it back, round after round snapping into its chest. It rolled against the ground and tried to stand again, undeterred and unthreatened.

Casings sprayed from the ejector on Tommy's rifle as the rounds rained down on the creatures.

Another, a woman, had a long, jagged claw stretching from her spine. Tommy shot her in the knee, making her tumble and crawl forward.

*They don't die.*

"My fucking arm!" Burns kept screaming, holding his arm as his fingers spasmed like they were on fire.

"They'll take your head if you don't move. The bullets aren't doing shit. Let's get the fuck out of here!" Tommy grabbed him by the shoulder and yanked, dragging him into a run. As they broke into a sprint, Burns turned to fire his rifle one-handed at a bellowing creature that got too close.

"Move!" Tommy screamed. "Move or we're dead!"

Once they were in the hallway, Tommy pressed the button on his comms and a burst of static filled the air. "Commander!" he screamed. "Do you read?" Static cracked and popped. "We turned the power back on, and we were attacked! Pax is dead! Repeat, *Pax is dead!*"

## 11

TEALSON WAS CALM AND QUIET, at least as much as he could be under the circumstances. Still, he would kill for a cigarette. He tried to shove the cravings to the back of his mind. He had a lot to think about. He'd just closed a transmission with Alice.

Alice had said she couldn't identify several organs, and the unconscious body didn't contain any lungs. The heart was also shriveled up and wasn't working, as if there was no longer a use for it.

Yet, the being still lived.

*Was 'lived' even the right word?*

He and his flight crew sat in silence, rolling the news through their heads.

"Son of a bitch," Tealson mumbled under his breath.

"Indeed," Bennie answered, raising his eyebrows. "I was wondering when you were finally going to speak, and *son of a bitch* seems to fit the situation perfectly."

"It doesn't have lungs, Bennie."

"I know; I heard." Bennie shrugged. "At least we got the lights on now, right?"

"What the hell kind of thing could be up and moving without lungs and no beating heart?"

"Russians," Bennie said flatly.

This finally got Tealson's attention as he slowly looked over at Bennie. "Russians? What are you saying, son?"

"The goddamn Russians did it," Bennie sneered. "I'm sure of it."

"That doesn't even make sense," Stalls cut in. "How could they do anything like that?"

Tanaka stayed quiet, looking down in contemplation.

"I don't know *how* they did it, but they did." Bennie pointed at Stalls. "You know it. Sabotage or something. This isn't natural. It was made in some KGB lab and weaponized. They're on a fucking space station after all. Nothing gets out here. Whatever the hell fucked them up was manufactured. This was sabotage for that big middle finger of a Mars station you mentioned earlier, Commander. Couldn't beat us in space, so they're going to knock us down a peg."

Tealson stared at Bennie. He wanted to tell Bennie he was full of shit. He *really* wanted to. . . but hell if that wasn't the best theory so far. He threw his hands up and sighed. "Who knows, Bennie? Maybe you're right."

"Commander," Tanaka said looking up. "I'm getting interference on our monitors."

"What?" Tealson moved over. "You kidding me? Don't I have enough problems without this piece of shit falling apart? Get Moller in here to take a look."

"My instruments are off too," Stalls said. "I'm not sure what's causing it. I've never seen it do this before." Stalls tapped her knuckles on the console. "They're all screwy."

"Dammit, I'll get DalBon in here, too." He moved to the comms and pressed a button. A burst of static popped on. "The hell? Moller, DalBon? Either of you read?"

*"Yeah I'm—"* The static sizzled. *"—need?"*

Tealson sighed and slapped the console. "I can't hear you for shit. Both of you get up to the bridge."

*"On—"* another burst. *"—now."*

"Goddamn Russians. They're doing something, I know they are."

75

Bennie shook his head. "I can see the headlines now—mysterious contagion on Felicity. Mars station abandoned."

Tealson swiped his hand through the air. "Do me a favor and cut the shit, Bennie."

Engineer Joseph DalBon showed up, rubbing his jaw. "What's the matter?"

Stalls pointed to her board. "The instruments are fucked."

DalBon came over and looked at them. "Well, hell, what do you want me to do about this? There's signal interference. You want me to go out and jiggle the goddamn antenna?"

Lacey Moller walked in. Her hair was pinned back, and she wore rectangle framed glasses. She was nervous—always nervous—and spoke softly. "Commander, I heard your transmission, but it wasn't clear."

DalBon pointed at Stalls's instruments and reported in an uncharacteristically serious tone. "Getting signal interference here, too. Whatever it is, it's hitting both the comms and our flight gear."

Moller blinked as she came closer. "Was the ship damaged, perhaps? Otherwise, it looks like something is jamming us."

"Goddamn Russians!" Bennie's eyes lit up. "*Told you.*"

"Bennie," Tealson sneered. "I told you to cut the—"

A transmission came bursting in. The communication was fractured and nearly incoherent, but the tone was clear. "*Com—*" It sizzled and cracked.

Frowning, Tealson looked the others over and pushed the comms. "Say again?"

Another transmission, clearly Pax, but Tealson couldn't understand him clearly. "*—reconnected—*"

Tealson looked up and everyone shook their heads. He pressed the comms again. "Can't hear a damn thing you're saying, Pax. Just bring it all back in."

The comms remained silent.

"That makes everything all the more fun, right?" Stalls grinned sarcastically.

Moller nodded. "It's the power. Must be." She bobbed her head.

"They turned the power on, and then the comms and instruments started reading interference? We'll just have to determine what's causing the interference and turn it off."

Tealson crossed his arms. "I'm thinking we just shut the whole damn thing off again and radio to Earth, tell them this is out of our pay grade."

"That could be dangerous, Commander," Moller said. "It's possible that cutting the power abruptly before is what triggered the water leakage. It's an old facility, and proper upkeep might not have been maintained."

DalBon shrugged. "Could be right. Maybe the water stopped flowing, and one of those pipes froze up and busted. Cut it again, and something that's cracked might just explode this time."

Tealson turned, putting his hands on his hips and looking out into the void. "This whole goddamn mission just keeps getting better and better, doesn't it? Hell with it, though. Let's get together and go take a look out there for our—"

A scattered transmission broke again. It was Tommy this time. "— *power came back on and—is dead! Repeat, Pax is—*" a long burst of silence and then another transmission that blared with gunfire. "—*still coming!*"

*Fuck me.*

DalBon frowned deeply. "Did he. . . did he just say Pax is dead?"

*Do something.*

"No, that's not what he said," Bennie said as he smiled awkwardly in disbelief. "The power shorted, I think. But—"

*Do something!*

Tealson's head snapped up, his body finally listening to his commands. "DalBon, go grab the rifles. Five of them. Meet us at the hatch."

"I think that—"

"*Double time!*" Tealson barked. "Bennie, Stalls, you two get this bird ready to launch. We're aborting mission. Tanaka!" He yelled to the technician. "Send me the schematics, *now.*"

"Roger," Tanaka replied.

Stalls spun around in her chair. "What are you going to do?"

Tealson already had the schematics up and was studying the route to the power room. "I'm going in."

IN THE MEDICAL LAB, Alice jumped as the lights turned on in the hallways and machines began to rattle to life.

*He did it. The power's back on.*

Even so, dread began to creep up her spine, and she was anxious for Tommy.

*Not just Tommy. All of them.*

She tried her best to focus once more on Lyndsay, still strapped to the table and sedated.

Elliot shifted uncomfortably near the door. "You know, we really shouldn't be in here with that *thing* for this long," he said. "It can't possibly be anything *but* bad for us. For all we know it's got invisible spores shooting out of its fucking forehead or some. . ."

*Dammit, Tommy, what's taking you so long? I'm going to kill this guy if you don't hurry back.*

". . .next thing you know you're crawling on the ceiling with tentacles coming out of your ass, screaming in another language. And—"

Alice interrupted. "It doesn't have lungs, Elliot. It doesn't have a beating heart, but it seems to be circulating blood. Anything could be possible with this. It could have infectious microbes that line your lungs when you breathe it in. That's why we didn't bring it onto the ship." She looked back down. "And I suggest you keep your helmet on."

Bartlet paced near Elliot and shook his head. "This whole thing is *fucked*."

A burst of communication came through their comms. "*Winters? El —*" Static sizzled, and they could hear nothing else.

Alice pressed the comm. "This is Winters, say again?"

"*—power—something is—Reeves.*"

Alice looked at Elliot and Bartlet, and her heart beat faster. The two men stared back, eyes wide.

"Commander?" she said into the comms. "We can't read you. Something is interfering with the signal."

"*Attacked. Something—*" the words were loud and clear before they crackled once more. "*Attacked Reeves. We—going to—get Reeves. We are going—get Reeves.*"

Her knees went weak, and she had to grab the table to keep from falling. Was she in a dream? None of this felt real. None of it could be. She looked to the creature, a husk of a woman who should have long since died, yet it still moved. It was a dream. It had to be.

*No. It's a nightmare.*

"*Do—read?*"

Elliot pushed his comms. "Confirmed. We heard you." Elliot was already starting to pick up the gear. "We're heading back."

"*Say—gin?*"

"Heading back," Bartlet screamed into the comms. "*We're heading back!*"

"*Negative,*" Tealson said, and as if Hell interceded, the next words were clear. "*Stay put.*"

Bartlet kicked a box, sending it flying. "Stay put? Fuck that. We should head back to the ship now."

"No wait-wait-wait!" Elliot sputtered, the panic clear in his eyes. "Don't you get it? They're going to come here and get us. We need to just—"

"That's not what they said." Bartlet shook his head, his voice booming. "They're going to get *Reeves*, not us. They told us to stay put because they don't know what the fuck they're doing."

Alice's teeth chattered. She watched the two men argue, but her mind was somewhere else. Something had kicked inside her and started up the playbox of old memories. Was it the burst of static or the commands of military men? She didn't know, and it didn't matter. Her breath came in sharp gasps as she remembered the fall of Tripoli. Men dying. Their heads sawn off in the street. Screams. So many screams. Men—just like Tommy—marched in front of waiting video cameras, their spirits broken as their captors knocked them to their knees and brandished serrated knives.

There was blood. So much blood. Men and women—torn apart by IEDs—were brought to her. Their lives hanging in her hands. She watched so many die. Saw the last of their moments.

A person's dying eyes were unlike any others.

*Beep. Beep.*

The sounds of the medical scan pulled her from the memories. Shuddering, she took a deep breath, a tear rolling down her face. She blinked and shook her head, refocusing on the here and now.

"Hey! This thing is moving! It's fucking moving!" Elliot yelled, his finger extended and pointing.

Alice looked up, and the creature was stirring from its tranqs, the tentacles beginning to squirm once more as it opened and closed its hand. "*This,*" it hissed, and opened its yellow eyes, looking across the room and settling on Bartlet. "*Thing.*"

"Hell with it." Bartlet came close and leveled his rifle at its brain. "I'm blowing its head off."

"No, wait!" Alice held her hand up, but Bartlet was already firing.

The rifle's sound was near deafening in the enclosed medical lab. It made Alice's ears ring, but she saw the round pop into the creature's head, bursting it open like over-ripened fruit. Snapping back on her neck, bits of rotted brain and chunks of skull slung across the room. Her head rocked forward, and wet pieces of flesh and soft tissue sloshed out of her open skull.

Jennifer leaned up, still not dead, but her head was open from the nose up.

*Oh my God.*

Alice stood, fixated on the creature as its jaw opened.

*It's still alive.*

"The hell?" Bartlet whispered, lowering the rifle as he watched it.

*"Hell,"* it hissed.

## 13

*NINE. We have nine.*

Braun counted the people who had survived the trek across the station. He had expected casualties, but. . .

*This is unacceptable.*

Twenty had gone into cryo. Fifteen survived to awaken. Nine now lived after their first encounter.

*Forty-five percent survival rate.*

Braun had tried to prepare them, but there was only so much they could have done with pieces of metal broken off chairs and makeshift gas can flame throwers.

They had gone silently, as silently as a group of fifteen frightened scientists and researchers could. All had seemed well as they looked around corners and opened doors.

But a sudden, loud banging had drawn Braun's attention to the back of the group.

A long, chubby creature approximately the size of a man's arm broke through an air duct, knocking the metal screen to the ground. It shoved out its pointed head and twisted toward them.

It had no eyes or ears, only a long, pointed face that peeled open as it screamed.

Something howled in the distance, and someone in the group took off running. Like a herd of wild animals, they all took to following, and Braun stayed with them, afraid not for the creatures that may lay behind...

...but the ones that may lie ahead.

The group stretched out, and as Braun rounded the corner, he saw that they had been chased directly into a trap.

*They planned this?*

He'd only given the thought a moment's consideration before he saw a creature snake into view. The top half of the creature was all that looked anything like a man. The rest looked like a long tentacle of exposed muscle that it slithered on. A long, jagged appendage had broken through the creature's head, and it dangled there until it quickly jabbed forward into a member of Braun's group, piercing his brain.

Other creatures, all terrifying and horrendous with little that still resembled humans, fell upon Braun's group.

The screams of the dying echoed in the halls as Braun commanded the others to retreat.

They made their way into a security room, then barred the door until the locks clicked. The creature jabbed at the door with its tentacle, but couldn't breach the steel-plated door. Braun blocked the window, and, in time, it moved on to find other prey. Unseen and forgotten. They were simple beings indeed.

However... Braun kept his eyes on the vent.

*And now we're down to nine.*

"Scheisse," he hissed.

Now, with time to breathe and consider, Braun rubbed his chin and deciphered what he knew about the creatures. He determined there were two classifications of beings here. Natives—the white-skinned, eyeless creatures that surely came through the gate, and infected—humans who had been exposed in some way.

*Elites and slaves.*

The elites had no eyes, so how they were able to locate prey was yet to be determined.

His leading theory was by sound.

Braun turned to the survivors and counted them once more. He did so without feeling or emotion, but as a gambler counts his cards.

"We'll be safe in here, right?" a man whispered, his tone unsure.

"No," Braun said flatly—he was done with useless conversation. He moved to a monitor and took a seat. The keyboard clicked as he input his credentials and opened up the resource monitor. A list of items— all in *danger* red—told him the severity of the situation.

Oxygen levels were depleting quickly. Water had erupted and was pouring into the station. Doors meant to be securely in lockdown were opened for unknown reasons.

The list of problems went on.

The lines went fuzzy. His eye whined loudly as the lenses began to rub. Mechanical eyes were not intended to go into cryosleep. He should have pulled them both out, but there had been little time . . .

*And you were afraid of what would have happened had you woken up blind and unable to find them again.*

It was true. Perhaps it was only a bit of dust or debris rubbing between the focal points. Braun walked over to a small mirror and pulled his eye out with pinched fingers. A dangling, braided cord connected to his optic nerves strung out, attached to the mechanical eye.

"Braun, get over here. We need to figure this out."

"*Busy,*" he said as he inspected the eye.

"This is a security room," another man said. "It's more secure than the cryo room. Tonya would have told them we were here. We just need to—"

"Tonya is dead," Braun said as he popped the lens off his eye. White lubricant leaked from it and dripped down his fingers.

"You don't know that," the man said, shaking his head. "She could have made it!"

"And if she did?" He turned to look at him with one functioning eye. "What then? Air pressure is low and leaking. Water is filling up around our feet." He puckered his pale lips and blew the inside of the lens before popping it back onto the eye. "Did you see the ship? Markings on that ship don't indicate a combat unit. They will be facing an alien threat with low-grade weapons. There is no secure room. There is no waiting. I'm sure the crew would die before they got here."

"Then we wait for those things to leave and go back to cryo," someone said.

"You don't get it, do you?" Braun shoved the eye back into his empty socket. "They turned the power back on. Those things are coming in. Even if you *somehow* got back to the cryo room and there were no creatures there, the water is going to fill up more. If one more thing breaks here, this whole place could freeze and crack our cryo beds. Did you not see Jessica Marie or James Seamone's dried corpse? All the moisture sucked from their bodies, dying while they slept?"

Some of the others in the room recoiled at the mention of their dead colleagues. It was true. It could have been any one of them, and it was a sobering fact.

"What do we do then?" Carter asked.

Braun tilted his head as if it was obvious and they should have all understood it by now. "We're going to meet them halfway."

"*No,*" the red-haired woman said hotly.

"No what?" Braun said, sighing as his eye whirred around and tried to calibrate.

"I'm not going out there again," she said. "I'm staying right *here*. I don't have a deathwish." Several others nodded in agreement.

"You say you don't have a deathwish," Braun began, "but I find you have a very humorous way of showing it."

"That depends on which camp you fall into, I suppose," said Leonard, whose spine had apparently grown back, as he stood near the red-haired woman. "I'm not so sure I think it's a great idea to go out there with a bunch of bullshit weapons either. Sounds like a pretty stupid idea, actually. None of us are trained fighters; we're white-coats, that's it."

*I don't have time for this.*

Braun took a step forward, his eye finally calibrated and locked in on the man. "Those things out there," he pointed at the door, "those *monsters* that *ate* our colleagues aren't concerned with what color your coat is. They're more interested in the taste of your insides, which happen to be the same no matter what your choice of wardrobe is. Now," he mimed drawing a line between himself and Leonard. Braun cleared his throat and spoke louder, "I am not a begging man, and I won't ask twice. I'll keep this simple: if you understand the dangers and futility of waiting here for rescuers who won't arrive, then stay. Otherwise, come with me."

Nobody moved for a few moments until finally one of the scientists, Michael Gardenier, stepped across the imagined barrier and reached over, grabbing a large hammer off a table. One by one, more of the group joined Braun and Michael in finding crude weapons until there were only three on the other side of the room.

"Good luck to you all," Braun said as he and his few followers stepped into the corridor.

## 14

"YOU WITH ME, BURNS?" Tommy asked as he carried Burns under the shoulders. The younger man was wheezing, and Tommy was nearly dragging him.

*His arm . . .*

The wound on Burns's forearm had strange, black ink that appeared to be spreading up his flesh. Tommy wasn't a scientist or a doctor—he didn't know how to identify a contagion—but the wound on Burns's arm. . .

*I'm sure no one has ever seen anything like that before.*

"*Hurts,*" Burns said in a strained voice. "*It hurts.*"

*He's going to turn into one of those things before this is all over.*

Tommy's instincts screamed fear and panic. *Drop him!* his nerves demanded. *Leave him before he kills you!*

But Tommy held on, grabbing Burns's good wrist and dragging it over his shoulder for more leverage. "Hold on, kid!"

Even with the wounded arm, Burns raised his rifle, firing an uneven blast that shook them both. The bullets peppered a human-like creature that had come up behind them, blowing off a leg and forcing it into a crawl.

"Keep it up, kid!" Tommy said between grunts. "Winters will fix you up. She will. You're going to be fine." Tommy kept talking, the words pouring out of his mouth as they trudged through the water.

"*Winters*," Burns said, his eyes rolling up into his head before he blinked and cleared them. He slung his rifle up and fired another burst behind them.

Tommy kicked something hard and solid in the water and stumbled, dropping his rifle. Burns came loose from him and hit the wall, holding himself upright.

"Fuck me!" Tommy screamed as he searched on hands and knees in the water for his rifle.

He glanced up to see Burns still firing, but he didn't look at what. He could feel them behind him, coming closer—their breath upon his neck, their teeth tearing his veins. The vision sent him into a panic, and he sloshed in the water until he found his rifle. He snatched it and got up on his feet.

Amidst the screeching and bellowing, there was something else from the other direction. Tommy looked up to see a woman coming around the corner wearing a scientist's jacket.

"*Wait! Wait!*" she screamed.

But it had been too sudden, and Burns was too afraid, too shell-shocked. A burst from his rifle lit her up.

Tommy was certain she wasn't infected.

She didn't get back up.

"Fuck! Stop!" Tommy screamed at Burns.

"Oh God, was that . . . " Burns's eyes were wide.

Tommy trudged over to the woman and pulled her up from the water. She opened and closed her mouth, spitting up blood and water as her eyes seemed to quiver in her head. She gagged out strange noises before going limp. Tommy let her body loose.

"Was she—"

"Yes," Tommy said, cutting him off. "But it doesn't matter. Not now." He yanked Burns's arm back onto his shoulder. "We have to move."

He saw one of the creatures round the same corner as the woman "Shit!" Tommy shouted as it cut them off.

*They're coming from all sides.*

Holding his rifle with one arm, Tommy unloaded a volley of bullets in its direction. His rifle kicked and jumped awkwardly in his hand from his improper grip, but the blasts slammed into the creature, making it dance before a round caught its soft head and blew pieces away in a spray of fleshy chunks.

He pulled in a breath and started dragging Burns again. "Let's go, Burns. You can do it." Tommy groaned and struggled through the water, bearing both his and Burns's weight. It was only an arm wound, but Burns was weakening.

*It's in his blood. Leave him.*

Tommy resisted; he couldn't. He groaned as he heard Burns whisper, "Another," before he fired off his rifle from behind them. Tommy didn't look back. If he did, he might just be forced to drop Burns.

The creature rose up from the water as they passed by it.

Tommy turned to look over his shoulder after hearing Burns croaked again. "Empty," Burns said in a strained voice, dropping his rifle. *"Incoming."*

A shrieking creature came up behind them. Tommy spun, causing Burns to lose what little footing he had and collapse into the water at their feet. Tommy leveled his rifle and fired. Rounds peppered the creature, rocking it back—but his rifle went empty as well.

He let go of Burns and turned the rifle over in his hands as the monster neared. Its jaw was gone, and its tongue licked out like a reaching tentacle. Its yellowed eyes squirmed in its skull to focus on Tommy as it groaned for meat, hands reaching with hundreds of prickly, needle-like vines squirming on its finger tips.

"Get away from me!" Tommy screamed like a lunatic as he batted it in the head with the end of the rifle. "Fuck off!" The impact knocked it sideways in a dazed stagger and nearly took the thing off its feet. Tommy screamed as he raised the rifle with both hands and chopped it down with an axe swing, collapsing its skull. The creature toppled forward, splashing water in the air. Tommy raised the rifle over his head and slammed it down again, pulping what was left of the creature's skull.

He huffed, exhausted, his muscles burning. "Come on Burns, we have to—"

The creature was rising again.

"*Fucking*—" Tommy roared once more as he raised the rifle up and slammed it down in a fit of rage. "*Die!*" But this time, the creature's wet fingers curled around the rifle stock and locked tightly. The small, needle-like vines in its fingers dug in. Eyes wide in panic, Tommy tugged hard, but the creature held tightly, and Tommy nearly pulled it to its feet.

*It won't die.*

There was no choice anymore. No chance of killing or slowing them. He just surrendered the rifle to the creature and grabbed Burns under the arms, dragging him away. He then saw the one that had tried to cut them off was skimming through the water. The fist-sized hole in its cheek and right eye didn't hinder its momentum as it clawed toward them.

*These things don't stop.*

*They just keep coming.*

The one with his gun was reaching up for Burns, intent to wrench him from Tommy's grasp.

"*Reeves!*" someone screamed. "*Reeves, where are you?*"

His eyes lit up, and Tommy screamed, "We're here! We're down here!"

The thing grabbed onto Burns's leg and used its hold to pull forward. Burns groaned and weakly kicked at it, but still it climbed up his body. Its jawless, pulped head moaned as it reached for his face, dripping inky-black saliva on Burns's suit and helmet.

Tommy dropped Burns again and came around, grabbing the creature from behind, yanking as Burns batted it with his hands. Even as Tommy struggled with it, he saw the water parting with the one clawing in front of them. A realization hit him.

*I'm going to watch this kid die.*

At that moment, Tealson rounded the corner with a rifle aimed. "He's here!" he screamed.

"Get it!" Tommy shrieked and looked at the water. "Fucking kill it!"

Five men came in. Tommy couldn't tell one from the other, each with a matching suit, but he was happy to have help.

"Reeves!" someone yelled, but Tommy couldn't see who as he struggled with the creature intent on tearing out Burns's throat.

Tommy yanked back, and it dug its fingers into the grooves of Burns's suit, dragging him along with it. It groaned as it leaned its crushed head down toward Burns's arm and dangled its tongue near the bleeding wound.

"Behind you!" Parker's deep voice boomed.

Tommy looked too late. Something barreled into him and slammed him into a wall. Burns screamed as Tommy's helmet cracked, the glass spider webbing. Claws raked across him, and he felt the tips begin to shred his suit. Grunting, Tommy kicked back with all the force he could muster, and the creature squealed and fell off. He turned around and came face to face with it.

A naked man with graying skin. Blue veins popped across his flesh, and his crotch hung openly in the air. He seemed to be in a perpetual, miserable state of gagging, with roots growing from his mouth— living roots that squirmed and bent in Tommy's direction. Red tears leaked from his eyes as they rolled around in his head.

*My God...*

Tommy froze. The pain upon the man's face and body was cruel and shocking, enough that it held him in place. The man groaned again, and more roots crawled out.

Tommy had nothing. He thought nothing. He was nothing. He only watched as it came for him.

"The fuck, Reeves?" came the bellowing voice of DalBon as he got close and unloaded his rifle, cutting the creature in half. "That lead in your brain slip down to your ass? Get up and move!"

*Snap the fuck out of it.*

Tommy looked over and saw two men firing into the one that had been clawing at Burns, while someone else dragged Burns away.

Another person was pumping rounds into the creature that had tried to cut them off.

DalBon kicked him. "Get off your ass!"

Fuzzy and unclear, Tommy nodded. He got up amongst the screams of *"They're not dying!"* and *"It's fucking got me!"* Everything seemed to slow as he looked around. Parker's sneering face lit up with each round of his rifle. The creatures jigged and twitched as the rounds perforated their bodies.

"Blow their fucking legs off!" Tealson ordered, and Tommy watched him as they aimed their rifles down and turned the creature's legs into red mist.

"I said fucking move, dumbass!" DalBon slapped the side of Tommy's helmet, finally clearing his head.

They started to run, two men carrying Burns with arms looped under his.

Tommy struggled to keep up, but a realization hit him. *"Winters?"* he huffed. "Where's Winters?"

Tealson shot a look back and then at Tommy. "She's not here. She's still in the med bay. We're heading back to the ship."

"We have to get her!" Tommy said.

"No, get back to the ship. I'm going to tell them to get their asses back." Tealson ignored Tommy as they all slowed. The other men looked around uncomfortably. Tealson hit his comms button. A burst of static came in. Tealson flinched from the noise but tried to shout over it. "Winters? Bartlet? Elliot? Do you read?"

Another burst of static, and Tealson shook his head. "Comms are down. We're going to have to get them." He pointed at Parker and DalBon. "You two strap up the kid. We're going to have to drag him back. Reeves, you—"

"No," Tommy shook his head as he grabbed Smith's gun from him, eliciting a cursed response. "It's too slow to drag Burns there. You all get back. I'll run in and get them."

"Reeves, we don't know how many more of those damn things there are. We're going to stay tight and—"

"I'm going," Tommy said, as focused and as stern as he could. "I'm going *right now*."

"Fuck it." Tealson threw his hand up. "DalBon, go with him."

"*Shit*!" DalBon cursed as he stepped up. "Let's get movin' then."

Tommy headed off with DalBon, jogging through the water as quickly as they could, silently praying that the others were okay—that *Alice* was okay.

# 15

ALICE SWALLOWED HARD, the lump in her throat feeling more like a literal fist squeezing her neck. She couldn't believe what she was looking at. Never in her wildest dreams had she imagined she'd actually be one of the first humans to contact another species. She knew deep in her core something terrible had happened here.

*Communication lost. . .*

Something terrible and something equally fascinating—it was strapped to the table in front of her. She stared in horror, the thing's face splayed open and displayed for all to see—yet it still talked. It still reacted. And even with its brain leaking from its skull . . .

*It must still be thinking.*

It felt like everything was happening in slow motion. Her mind reeled as Bartlet and Elliot shouted on either side of her. The blasts of Bartlet's gun rang in her ear.

Crazed with rage and fear, Bartlet screamed, "Fucking—" He unloaded the gun, the blasts blowing apart all that remained of its head and neck. "—die!"

Its body threw back, and the medical table skidded against the floor.

Elliot yawned wide, popping his jaw and blinked his eyes to try and stop the ringing in his ears. "Goddamn!" he said, shaking his head. "The hell, man? Stop! It's tied down to a table! And you're gonna—" He stopped to move his jaw around. "You're gonna make me deaf! Let's just get the hell out of here. When the hell are they going to get here?"

"I don't know," Alice said. "You heard them just as well as I did. They told us to stay put."

"*Fuck* that." Bartlet paced the room, shaking his head. He looked down at the ammo counter on his rifle. "I'm getting out of here. Like—"

"Shut up!" Alice hissed. *"Look!"* She pointed at the thing on the table. With its head blown off, the restraint around its neck was ineffective. The sloppy mess that was its neck slid from the collar as it leaned up, ragged bits of its clothes falling loosely.

It pulled at its restraints, shaking back and forth in a futile effort to get out, *to get at them.*

Alice stumbled back in terror, her mind still working on the horror in front of her.

*How does it think without a brain? How does it even know we're here without eyes or ears?*

Bartlet made a sound like he had something caught in his throat, low at first, then eventually finding its place as a full-on guttural scream. She'd heard a sound like that before. From a man in Tripoli who had stumbled upon a friend's head in the street.

It was painful to the ears.

Elliot and Alice backed up, while Bartlet stood his ground, rifle aimed low. At that moment, she wasn't sure if he would drop it and fall to his knees, or. . .

He snapped the rifle up and aimed it. This time when he pulled the trigger, Alice was ready. She blocked the sides of her helmet and crouched to the floor closing her eyes as Bartlet fired.

*Over and over and over.* The words played in Alice's mind until each bullet seemed to whisper it to her. *And over again.*

She heard the table crash to the floor over the sounds of firing.

"Fuck you!" Bartlet yelled. He'd blasted a hole through its chest and another through its bicep—the impact so forceful that the entire table had fallen over with the creature still strapped to it.

The room went silent, except for the ragged, adrenaline-fueled breaths from the three of them. The table had fallen away from them and made it impossible to see if the thing was still moving.

*Is it. . . ?*

Nobody spoke, and as they stood and collectively gathered their breath, Alice heard a sound—small at first, but *growing.* A screeching sound, almost like nails on a chalkboard. She felt her face drain of color as she watched the table start turning slowly.

*Holy shit.*

Somehow it had gotten a hand free. A finger had been blown off, but the rest of the digits worked fine. With a long, slender arm, it reached out onto the floor and tried to pull. The hand squeaked across the floor without traction, leaving a copper-brown, bloody smear. It tried again, this time digging its nails into the groves of the floor and dragging the table screeching along with it.

"It won't. . ." Bartlet choked out, defeated. "It won't die."

By the sound of Bartlet's voice, Alice was sure he'd be haunted by this sight every night as he went to sleep for the rest of his life.

*How do you kill it? Think, Alice, the brain didn't matter at all. It's all over the walls.*

Elliot stepped past them, having yanked a computer monitor off a desk and hurled it at the creature. The monitor slammed into it, knocking it back farther. He then grabbed a chair and threw it at the weakened creature. Bartlet and Alice watched as Elliot huffed and tipped a table over top of it.

It was pinned in place, so they couldn't see it anymore.

Huffing, Elliot asked "What do we do?"

Alice could read the desperation in his eyes. Elliot was *terrified,* and it showed.

"Whatever is keeping this thing going, it has to be somewhere in the chest," Alice murmured. Shaking her head in disbelief, she pointed at the pile. "Its goddamn brain is gone, but it's still alive!"

From behind them, something beat on the door.

"Fuck!" Bartlet shouted, finally snapping out of his daze as he aimed the gun at the door. "There's more of them!"

Elliot held his hand up. "That's not one of them. Put your gun down!" He walked over to the wall and pressed a button to open the door. Tommy and DalBon were there, looking haggard and exhausted.

Bartlet looked down at the floor. "*Shit.* I'm losing my fucking mind."

"Ain't we all?" DalBon came in, sloshing water. He thumbed back to the flooded corridor. "You assholes just had one that was tied down. We had a bunch over there, and one of those things was running around with its dick hanging out and dragging all over. What kind of stupid-ass space zombie walks around with its dick hanging out?"

"Cut the shit, DalBon," Tommy said, shaking his head and breathing deep. He tried to catch his breath. "But he's right, there's more of them out there. This place has completely gone to hell." The glance he shot at Alice said more than words could ever say.

*I love you.*

"*Tommy,*" Alice said, dropping any formality as she moved closer to him, grabbing him for a hug. "I'm glad you're okay." She squeezed him, and he squeezed back, making her feel safe, if only for a moment.

He sighed as he held her. "Leave the gear. We're aborting the mission. Let's get the hell out of here."

"I don't get a hug?" DalBon shrugged and looked across the room. "Bring it on in, Bartlet." He motioned for the other man to come closer.

Bartlet huffed and stepped past DalBon to look outside. "There could be more soon. We need to get the hell out of here."

"Where the hell is it anyway?" DalBon frowned and scanned the room. He sounded calm, but his eyes spoke stress.

"Go dig it up, if you want." Elliot pointed to the pile it was beneath. "Genius over there blew it apart till there wasn't much left but a torso, but it kept crawling."

"Where are the others?" Alice asked, afraid of what they might say.

"We got attacked down there. Some of those things came right out of the water." Tommy's voice lowered. "They killed Pax. Burns got hurt too. One bit him and took a whole chunk out of his arm. He's with Tealson now. We had to shoot a lot of those fucking things. They still almost got us. They don't die easy."

"We know," Alice glanced at the pile. "Bartlet took its head clean off, and it was still moving." She shook, as if she wasn't sure about what she was about to say. "It's not a disease. A disease doesn't do *that* to you. I think we've found aliens, Tommy. Fucking aliens. It's unbelievable. Nobody has ever reported anything like this from anywhere we've been as a species. And yet here we are. . ."

"Can we please get the hell out of here?" Elliot moaned and looked at the floor. "Pax. . . Hell, I just don't want to be next."

The chair on top of the creature on the floor moved. It got the edges of its fingers out, still desperately trying to get at them.

"Shit. . ." DalBon whispered, taking an involuntary step back.

"At a loss for words, DalBon?" Elliot retorted, his words a little bitter. "Try having to be stuck in a room with it for no clear goddamn reason. I always seem to get fu—"

"This isn't about you, Elliot," Tommy interrupted. "It's bigger than just you, believe it or not."

"I'm done with this horseshit," Bartlet said, glancing back and then looking down both ends of the hallways. "Let's have this conversation on the ship."

"What a wonderful idea," Elliot said and kicked off the wall he'd been leaning against.

"Yeah, okay, let's go," Tommy said.

"All right," Alice said. She paused in the doorway, looking back at the pile on the floor. Her skin prickled even then, but part of her—a strange, curious part—pitied how pathetic the creature was.

They hurried back to the ship, passing through the doors and into the docking bay.

"Give me a hand," Tommy said as he motioned for DalBon and Bartlet to help him drag the doors closed. With a little effort, the three of them were able to close and lock them into place.

Parker stepped from the ship and motioned for them. "Winters, come on! We got Burns up here. He's waiting for you."

The group got into the ship's loading bay, and the doors locked on either side of them as they all stood in the tight room.

*"Prepare for decontamination,"* the ship's A.I. announced.

Hot, red lights pulsed for a solid ten seconds, then air jets blasted the room.

*"Decontamination, successful,"* the ship told them. *"Thank you and have a nice day."*

Slowly, the entrance to the ship door rose, and Alice instantly heard Burns screaming from the medical bay.

"Fuck, it hurts!"

Alice rushed down the hallway, not caring to wait for anyone else as she got into the room. Tanaka was there with a medical mask over her mouth and white gloves on trembling hands. She poured a disinfectant over the bite wound. Burns was still in his suit, head and all, but it was shredded open in places, exposing skin.

"Burns," Alice said as she came in. "Let me see it."

Tanaka backed up, and Burns showed her the wound on his arm. "It fucking hurts, Winters. God, please give me something for the pain at least. I can feel it inside me."

It had been a small bite, but there was something strange about it. The flesh and meat in his arm seemed like it was. . . *moving.*

*Nerve damage? Muscle tension?*

She looked back at Tanaka and pointed at a locker "Grab the red kit—over there with the infectious disease supplies."

"I'm gonna—gonna . . ." Burns hurriedly pulled his helmet off, the clasps popping as he flipped them up, and vomited into it. *"Sorry,"* he wheezed out.

"What the hell is wrong with him?" Elliot asked over Alice's shoulder.

Alice shot a glance back, seeing Tommy in the doorway and a few others behind him. "Get out!" she yelled at Elliot. "Everyone besides Tanaka! Get out and close the door!"

"It's going to be all right, Burns," Alice said in a low voice, waiting for Tanaka to bring her the kit. "Stay with us, Burns. You hear me?"

Burns nodded and slowly got back to his feet. "I'm good. . . I'm good."

*No, you're not.*

"You're going to be fine," she said as she opened the kit and started preparing the medicine. "Just fine."

He leaned over to throw up into his helmet again.

## 16

TEALSON HURRIED to the command room. He pulled his helmet off and hurled it at the ground in a fury.

"Pax?" Bennie said, his eyes wide.

"He's dead," Tealson answered, not bothering to meet his eyes. "Same with everyone else in that goddamn place."

Bennie went silent.

"Let's get the hell out of here," Bartlet shouted from down the hallway, and Tealson saw no reason at all not to comply.

He looked at a vid-screen and saw Alice in the med bay with Burns. The kid was puking his guts up as Alice pumped something into his veins with a syringe.

*Just a comms repair. Fucking Hell on Mars is what it is.*

"You got us prepped?" Tealson asked Stalls as he took his chair.

"All systems go, Commander," she said, not taking her eyes from her dash. "But my instruments are still coming in with clear misreadings."

"So you're half-blind. Can you get the bird in the air or not, Lieutenant Stalls?"

*"Sir, yes, sir,"* she spat back.

"Then get us the fuck out of here."

"Amen," Bennie said as he worked over his preparation controls.

Tealson leaned forward and pressed a button on the screen, using the loudspeaker rather than the comms radio, *"Everyone get strapped down. Departure in five minutes."*

---

ALICE DID everything she could to help Burns. He was strapped to the table now. He'd been so weak that he'd needed both Alice and Tanaka to help him lie down.

A full syringe of tranquilizers put him out, and Alice connected an IV drip to help fight back any possible infection.

*Any known infection.*

She wheeled over a mobile vid-screen and turned on the power, her hands shaking slightly. She'd been trained for this, sure, but it was never easy seeing someone this young hurt. Burns was practically just a kid, and the fact he'd been bitten by an unknown species made it even worse.

Tealson's voice boomed over the intercom: *"I need everyone strapped in. Two minutes to take off."*

"Winters. . ." Tanaka said as she glanced toward the exit.

"You're right. It'll have to wait," Alice said. She looked down at Burns, feeling sorry for him as he mumbled to himself. He was feverish, and his hair was plastered to his forehead in a sweaty mess.

*Dammit.*

Alice hung her head and sighed.

They walked to the door, which opened automatically on their approach. Tommy was waiting for them, clearly anxious. He straightened when he saw her.

"Come on," he said, reaching out to take her hand. "We'll be back to check on the kid in a few minutes. It won't hurt for him to have some rest in the meantime. Let's go, though; we have to hurry."

"Yeah, you're right," she nodded. They hurried to the lockdown room where they got seated and strapped in. Everyone except for the flight crew was there, but there were two empty chairs.

*Burns and Pax.*

"God, this is terrible, Tommy," Alice said, hanging her head. "This wasn't supposed to happen. We didn't sign up for this."

Tommy sighed. "No. . . but it's over." He took her hand in his and gripped it tightly.

She thought of the irony, visiting another planet and not even getting to set foot on its surface.

*Some easy communications check.*

She was just glad to be leaving.

---

TEALSON SAW a bead of sweat roll down Stalls's face. She was nervous. They all were.

*You can do it, Stalls.*

Stalls puffed her cheeks out and held the operating gear. She stared at the docking bay's wide doors. "Get those goddamn doors open for me, Bennie."

*Click-click.* That was the loud and audible snap of Bennie flipping a switch, but it had an extra layer of fear atop it for Tealson.

"Commands unresponsive," Bennie said. "It's the damn interference. We're going to need to use a manual crank on those doors."

"God-in-heaven," Tealson hissed. He reached over to the ship loudspeaker and hit the button. "Parker, you there?"

A few moments later, the loadmaster responded, "*Yes, sir.*"

"You know how to manually operate the ship bay doors?"

This time, the reply buzzed in with more trepidation. "*Yes, sir, I do.*"

"We need you to head off ship. We're getting signal interference to the door. We need you to operate it manually."

"Two-man job, sir." Bennie said.

Tealson nodded to Bennie and hit the comms again. "Take Smith with you. Double time it."

"*Yes, sir,*" Parker said, but Tealson heard Smith start to curse just as the signal cut off.

Stalls looked out the ship's windows. "Hate this whole damn place," she whispered. "Just let me get my damn wings in the air."

"Don't worry." Tealson stepped out of his chair and walked closer to the window. "You're going to get your chance to dazzle me with your piloting skills soon enough."

"They just opened our ship doors now, sir," Bennie said.

"Where are they now? I don't see shit," Tealson said, more to himself than anyone else.

"There!" Stalls said, pointing. Parker and Smith were jogging from the ship and to the bay doors.

"*Hurry your asses up,*" Tealson mumbled.

Parker stopped mid-jog and pointed to something. Smith stopped alongside him, and they both looked.

"What the *fuck* are they doing?" Stalls asked, her eyes wide.

Tealson shook his head in irritation.

"It's one of those things!" Bennie said, the alarm in his voice clear. "Something got in here! I'm going to close the ship doors." He was already reaching to flip the switch.

"Negative." Tealson was tight and focused, staring at them. "Hold that."

"Don't get those doors open, and I'm going to have to go through them." Stalls shook her head, biting her lip.

"You *insane?*" Bennie asked in disbelief. "That could rip a wing off!"

"You two *shut up,*" Tealson said, and they both went silent. He looked out the window again.

Parker jogged off while Smith moved to the door commands. They looked like they were yelling at each other, but it wasn't clear about what. Moments later, Parker came running back into view, waving an arm at the ship as he moved to the door commands.

Tealson finally let out a breath, deflating in his chair as the doors began to rise. A gust of wind sucked out of the room as the bay opened to the martian atmosphere and the room depressurized. Parker and Smith jogged back.

"Door's closing, sir." Bennie looked back and gave a thumbs up. "We're good to go."

"Lieutenant Stalls?" Tealson asked.

"Sir?"

"Get us the fuck off of Mars."

# 17

MIKE BURNS COULD FEEL straps biting into his skin. He knew he'd been strapped to a medical table inside the belly of the *Perihelion*. A full syringe of *shut the hell up and sleep so it doesn't hurt so bad* was flowing through his veins.

Today was the worst day of his life.

It wasn't because of the throbbing bite wound on his arm, though that was certainly horrible. It also wasn't because he had a faint awareness of what was happening around him, something that shouldn't be happening with so many drugs mixed into his system.

He certainly would have hoped the drugs were working the way they should be. That he wasn't there at all, but in some distant dream. A dream he could just wake up from after they were safely back on course.

But that wasn't going to happen, and it also wasn't the worst part of his day, though it certainly was a contributing factor.

No. The worst thing was that he could feel it *moving* inside him.

His eyes fluttered open, blinking rapidly as he let out something between a groan and a gasp. *"Inside,"* he whispered to an empty room. *"Inside me."*

He hadn't felt it before. It might have been small, but now it was strange. It was almost as if he was seeing through its eyes. Understanding what it knew, and becoming more than he was.

When it bit him, the eyeless creature injected a parasite into his blood. It didn't need to eat him.

Not like when it had Pax.

Of course, that hadn't stopped the mindless others, the ones that were like what Burns would soon become. They certainly would have taken his flesh if given the opportunity. He understood. They were hungry.

The hunger was growing inside him too.

But he didn't like it. He didn't want it. He struggled against it, pulling against the restraints. "*Inside,*" he said again in a hoarse whisper. "*It's inside me.*"

He could feel the little tendrils growing out of the hunger deep inside him, snaking and crawling through his circulatory system. Twining between his muscles and growing down his fingers. Spiraling around his ribs as they twisted into his lungs and heart.

"*Get.*" Burns barely choked the whisper out as he felt it climbing up his spine. "*It.*" Snaking around his neck, dozens of little tendrils attached themselves. "*Out.*" They crawled into his brain, and he felt blood drip down his nose.

Burns never had much of a future. Prospects of college were never that appealing to him. He had been directionless and floating in the world, unsure of *what comes next* in his life. His scores had been just good enough to get into Orbital Corps and avoid having to sign up with the Marines like his father had wanted. He wanted to see space, but even that got old and tiring after so long.

But for all he was, and ever could have been, he was nothing now —only a tool for another being.

Thoughts and images filled his mind. Creatures and places that couldn't possibly exist, yet somehow he knew to be real. It shattered his sanity to look upon and drove what little remained of Burns mad.

Burns—or rather the shell of him—barked laughter. He whipped his head back and forth in his restraints, gnashing his teeth as he did so. "*Inside.*" The word—a hollow reflection to an understanding he no longer had. *"Me. Inside."* His gnashing teeth clipped his tongue, and he bit it off. The pain meant nothing to him as he spit it out. *"Me."*

His skin split open like a weak seam as a root grew from it. Pointed and twisting, it curled in the air. *"Inshid."* The word was also twisted with no tongue to form it. *"Me."* He leaned up, straining so hard the restraints groaned. Clenching his teeth together, the whispers of another being—not inside him but distant—spoke to him. It did not speak with words, but still he understood.

The hunger was upon him too. It demanded focus.

"Oh my God!" someone yelled and then gasped. Who it was—or what the words meant—no longer mattered to Burns.

Burns turned, his eyes straining in his skull to see as he pulled against the restraints.

He was hungry.

# 18

In orbit above Mars, Tealson undid his safety harness and waited for the artificial gravity to kick in. Once it had, he stood up. "I'm going to report mission failure. You two plot us a course back to Earth."

"Yes, sir, preparing exit of Mars' orbit." Stalls said, her hands working across keys.

"Confirmed. Plotting return course," Bennie replied.

Tealson flipped the ship's loudspeakers. "All crew clear from take-off. Go ahead and stretch your legs."

"Sir, looks like the instruments are good again," Stalls said, looking over her shoulder. "Whatever the hell was interfering, it must be on Mars."

"Roger that." Tealson rubbed his temples. He needed a shot of whisky, a few migraine pills, and about twelve hours of sleep.

He walked out into the ship, heading toward his living quarters—a privileged cabin located away from the rest of the crew.

"Commander!"

Tealson turned to see Parker coming up to him, a pack of cigarettes in one hand. "Found this in the bay." He held it out. They were Reds. Tealson's favorite brand.

Tealson took them and looked it over. "This was what you were looking at?"

Parker nodded. "Figured I'd grab it for you."

"Appreciate it." Forcing a smile, Tealson said in dark humor, "Maybe today ain't so bad after all."

With an empathetic frown and nod of his head, Parker turned and headed back down the ship.

Chuckling so as to keep from screaming, Tealson headed to his quarters, his knees feeling weak. His cheek twitched, fighting to form a sneer, but he kept his face stiff and emotionless. Each step upon the metal grating of the ship's floor seemed louder than it had ever been. His hands balled into fists, tightening as he came to his door.

"Access. Tealson."

The door to his room slid open, and the computer spoke, "*It is recommended that you receive two hours of—*"

"Shut the fuck up," Tealson said in a flat, humorless tone. He pulled a cigarette out of the pack. He looked it over for a moment and remembered how it was nearly all he could think about a few hours ago. His hand began to shake, and he watched it idly as he involuntarily crushed the cigarette. His eyes stayed focused and steady, as was his breathing.

It was just his hands that trembled with cowardice.

He dropped the pack on the floor and took a moment to stare out his window into the void, clenching his hands open and closed. As his nerves settled, he leaned down and picked the pack up again, pulling out a cigarette and swiping the lighter off the desk.

He lit it and took a puff, letting the smoke fill his lungs before he blew it out. He took two more drags before he sat down in front of his console.

The cigarette dangled from his lips as he typed in his credentials and opened up a communications link with Earth.

He pressed the record button and then sat in silence, which seemed to drag on forever. A red light blinked as he considered what to say.

*This is CO James Tealson. We're heading back, just letting you know. Oh, and you sent us to the portal of hell on this mission, thanks for that. Eat shit.*

He cleared his throat and plucked the cigarette out, its smoke snaking up as he focused on the screen. "Commanding Officer James Tealson broadcasting. I'm sending in a report from aboard the *Perihelion* as we flee the surface of Mars where my crew has been attacked by... well, I don't know exactly what." Pausing, he took another drag. Working over how to describe what he saw, but all he could see in his mind was red. "We encountered..."

Another long pause.

"*Unknown entities.*" He stopped again and stared into space. "*Non-human entities.*"

His heart thumped in his chest, and the cigarette smoldered between his fingers.

"Mars Felicity station is in critical failure. All personnel assumed lost. We have injuries as well as one casualty. Mission is a failure. Repeat: Mission is a failure. We are aborting and currently exiting Mars' orbit." He stared into the screens, wondering if anyone would believe him—if they all would think he was insane. "We are aborting mission."

He pressed the button again to stop the recording.

Now there was nothing to do but wait. He did so in a half-cata-tonic state as his mind tried to process what had happened. This far out, it could be five minutes or more between relays from Earth.

After a time, a green icon light popped onto his screen. He clicked it, and a voice came on.

"*Situation acknowledged, Commander Tealson. Request for abort is denied. Please await further instructions.*"

*Denied?*

His heart beat faster now, and tension clawed up his neck. He dropped the cigarette to the floor, leaving it to sizzle upon the metal as he leaned in, pressing the red button.

"Earth Command, I say again. We have encountered unknown, non-human entities. We have received one casualty and have one wounded. All personnel on Mars Felicity are likely dead. Repeat: All personnel on Mars Felicity likely dead." He itched all over, his chin twitching as he struggled for the words to make them understand. "We are a reassigned cargo crew. We are not a combat unit. We are not properly armed to engage. Abort mission requested."

He clicked the button again and hit send. It was only then he realized he'd dropped his cigarette, and so he smashed his heel into it.

Agonizing minutes passed as he clasped his hands together, staring at the screen and willing it to turn green.

Five minutes after his second transmission, it finally did.

*"Commander Tealson? This is Earth Command, Richard John Roles, mission specialist and intelligence coordinator for—"*

"I don't care who you are, you snooty cunt!" Tealson screamed at the recording as it continued to speak.

*"—your request to abort is denied. I understand the situation—"*

"Like fuck you do!"

*"However, have you encountered any living within the ship? Have you located cryo cells? Did you engage while in CAGs with weapons ready status? Please report mission status."*

*Dead. All dead. Mission failure. Aborting before we're all dead too.*

Tealson stopped to consider, a thousand thoughts racing through his mind all at once, each struggling to come out of his lips. The Mars Felicity base was untenable. They didn't have the training for this. They didn't have the weapons or the man power.

*Logistics. That's all we are. Logistics and goddamn repairmen.*

*Pawns.*

But for all he thought and all he was, Tealson was a soldier and loyal to his duty.

He pressed the record button.

"We have not encountered cryo pods. We engaged in all atmosphere suits. Our CAGs are in storage in the ship but are functional." He hesitated, rubbing his temples before he spoke. "One member of our crew encountered a woman during an attack. She was accidentally shot. She appeared to be Felicity personnel. Repeat. Felicity personnel encountered alive." He sent the message and waited.

And as the silence filled his room, his thoughts began to torture him again.

*We're going to die here. Just like everyone else. Just because we were the quickest crew ready and able to be sent on a seven-month trip to Mars. We're going to die because we were convenient.*

"Sir?" Tanaka said, her voice buzzing on Tealson's room comm. He looked once more to the screen, still minutes to go, and then leaned over and hit the comms button.

"Yes?"

*"Lieutenant Reeves is here. He wants to see you. He wants to report."*

"It'll have to wait," Tealson said. A moment later he reconsidered and pushed the comms again. "Actually, send him in."

*"Confirmed."*

Moments later, the door behind Tealson opened, and in stepped Tommy. "Lieutenant Reeves," Tealson nodded in his direction. "How's Burns? What's the verdict with him?"

"We don't know yet, sir," Tommy said, "Officer Winters is checking him now. She's got him doped up pretty good. What I *can* tell you is that he's lucky to be alive."

Tealson sighed. He wasn't sure he'd use the word *lucky* just yet. They weren't out of the water yet, not even close. He decided to keep those thoughts to himself. "Thanks, Reeves," he said. "Keep me updated on his status. How about everyone else? Any more injuries?

"No, sir."

Tealson nodded. Tommy kept standing there as if he were waiting for something. "Sir?" he asked. "Please tell me we're getting out of here. Please tell me we're going home."

Tealson couldn't look him in the eyes. Turning away, he faced the vid-screen. The message had yet to come. "That is yet to be determined," was all he could manage.

"Sir?" Tommy said skeptically. "Are you saying—"

Tealson kept his gaze on the screen, awaiting the green blink of the icon. "I'm not saying a goddamn thing right now, Reeves."

"We can't go back in there. There was something there. . . different than the infected people. The thing that bit Burns? It wasn't human. It was like—like it crawled out of hell. A fucking *demon*. There was nothing human about it. It didn't even have eyes."

"Confirmed," Tealson said flatly. The green message icon blinked on.

"Sir, we have to—"

"*Do what we're told. Our duty. Obey orders.*" He rolled his head up to meet Tommy's gaze. His eyes were hard, challenging. "Is that what you were going to say, Reeves?"

Tommy's mouth opened. It was obvious he wanted to say something in opposition, but he stopped and considered. "Sir, yes, sir."

"Lieutenant," Tealson said, his eyes unblinking. "Return to the bay and inform the crew that we are awaiting further orders."

"Yes, sir." Tommy snapped his head up and turned out of the room.

After he left, Tealson pushed the button, every muscle inside him squeezing tight.

"*Confirmed,*" Richard John Roles said, as if it were nothing at all. "*You are cleared to obtain CAGs and treat Felicity as an active war zone. However, mission priority has changed. It is mission critical that you locate and retrieve a resident of Felicity. Will Braun. Locate him or confirm his death.*" Roles breathed deep before dropping all military formalities. "*I'll be frank with you here, Commander Tealson. Will Braun is actually the war criminal, Waeheall von Braun—*"

"What?" Tealson hissed out loud as the recording continued.

"*—repositioned on Felicity after his history was revealed to the public. I'm sure you can understand why. He is critical to the war effort and needs to be recovered at all costs. It's a heavy price to put upon you and your crew, but your country needs you, Commander Tealson, now more than ever.*

*Braun was the brainchild of several top-priority projects we had nestled up there in Felicity. Losing him would be a great wound to us. And, for all we know, the goddamn Russians are the ones likely responsible for all of this. So, I repeat, mission abort denied. Mission priority, locate and retrieve Waerheall von Braun or confirm his death. And find us someone who can tell us what the hell happened there.*"

Waerheall von Braun. Tealson knew the name. Just like everyone else, he'd watched the trials fifteen years back. Words like "*mistake*" and *"it will never happen again"* were uttered by members in the highest levels of government.

*Typical.*

But it didn't matter. That was then, and this is now. The country needed Waerheall von Braun, and, at the moment, Tealson and his crew were the only ones capable of doing anything about it.

"Seven months," he uttered the words aloud to the empty room. That's how long it would take to get another group here—a combat unit suited for this kind of work.

Seven months, and Will Braun would assuredly be dead, if he wasn't already.

*But what about your crew if you go back? Are you certain you can keep them safe?*

It didn't matter. Nothing mattered except for the mission. He stood up and gazed out into the void once more. As he looked, he felt a peculiar sense, like he was falling.

Down. Down. Down.

But the fall never hurt anyone.

It's the impact that kills you.

CAGs—Combat Armor Gear—would be down in storage. They were surplus and a generation or two older than the current ones now being utilized in the Libyan War and Venezuelan conflict. The fact that Orbital Corps carried them at all was an artifact of a perceived space war with the Russians that never happened.

However, the Commander's CAG was always stored in his quarters. Tealson looked over to the locked closet that housed it. He'd never opened it, because he hadn't ever had a reason to.

The last time he'd even been through refresher training was five years ago.

"Hate these damn things," he had remarked to the course instructor. "Always tight in the crotch."

He stood in front of his closet, his shoulders drooping with the weight of responsibility. He spoke, "Commander Tealson, confirming CAG retrieval."

*"James Romulus Tealson."* The computer said as the light on the lock

turned green. *"Confirmed."* The locks clicked, and the doors slowly opened.

The CAG was still polished and clean, but dents from its previous use were clear. He couldn't help but wonder if anyone had ever died in it.

The armor would be heavy. The systems would boost personal strength and protect from environmental threats. It might just be enough. They might make it out.

*Maybe.*

With all it was, it would take an assistant to fit it on. Tealson hit the comms button. "Tanaka?"

"Yes, sir?" Tanaka replied.

"Please come in here. I need help fitting on my CAG."

Moments of silence passed, in which Tealson was sure that the inclinations were weighing on her. "Confirmed."

---

ALICE'S HEART FLUTTERED. She'd been sitting on a cold, metal bench waiting for Tommy with a few others. When he came back, his face drained and pale, he shook his head.

"What did he say?" she asked. "What are we going to do?"

Tommy shook his head. "I don't have a damn clue. Tealson's still up there talking with Earth command. They might end up making us wait here to greet a squad of marines."

*"Shit,"* whispered Peter Becks. "We'll be sitting here for seven or eight months, floating around in orbit. We even got the rations for that shit?"

Smith thumped his head back to the wall. "We do if we sleep in cryo shifts and they resupply us." Smith shook his head, grinning sardonically. "That ain't it, though. It's not about greeting no marines. They want us up here in quarantine. Just think about it. Unknown contagion. Would you advise bringing that shit back to Earth, Winters? Hell no. We're a multi-million-dollar science experiment now."

Alice shook her head at him, but truthfully she couldn't disagree. She wasn't sure what had infected the Mars Felicity group. It could have been anything.

*And if you were smart, you would have left Burns back there.*

There it was. The fear speaking, but it did have a very rational sense to it. They didn't know what they were dealing with. Until they did, it was her responsibility to make sure that she didn't open it up to a wider population.

She didn't want that responsibility, though. All she wanted to do was crawl into a dark corner and let someone else take over.

*Don't say that. You're the doctor here. If this is a viral break out, you are going to be in charge.*

"—you can bet your ass it's all about money. We're just names on paper against a weighted dollar sign." Smith had apparently kept talking, but Alice had tuned him out. "That's why I keep saying—"

Alice stood up. "I'm going to go check on Burns. Better to be useful than to sit here wallowing in self pity."

"I'll go with you," Tommy said, still holding his helmet in one hand.

She thought about it for a moment and shook her head. "You don't need to. Why don't you just go take a rest?"

Tommy reached down and squeezed her hand, unconcerned with hiding it. PDA protocol had been shot to hell and no one cared anymore. "I'll go with you."

She nodded and brushed a strand of her hair from her face. They walked together down to the lab. "Access," Alice said at the door, and it slid into the wall.

They walked in, and the door slid closed behind them. Burns sat trembling in the corner. His head swiveled in their direction.

"*Inshid,*" he said in a demonic-sounding voice. "*Me.*"

"Oh my God!" Alice yelled, just as the long, wet tendrils slithering from Burns's body came alive in the air. They lashed about with a power she hadn't seen with the woman from the med bay.

*They're fresh and not starved.*

That was an odd thought, but it came to her all the same. The tendrils whipped about, smashing glass and knocking over the trays in the med room. One snagged against something on the ceiling, and it pulled with such force that Burns's whole table groaned.

"Get behind me!" Tommy yelled and stuck his arm out in front of Alice.

Another forceful yank from the reaching tendrils and Burns's bed snapped completely off from its base with a loud crunch of bending metal. Everything clattered to the floor, and Burns came up to his feet quickly, one wrist still strapped to the metal bed.

"*Inshid*," he slurred like an alcoholic deep into the bottle. "*Me*."

Alice saw his eyes then, wide and still human as dozens of prickly veins streaked toward the center of his pupils.

"Access!" Alice screamed to the door, and it slid open. She could already see the other crew members running down to investigate. She looked back, and Burns was already on them, faster than she could have possibly imagined.

He'd dragged the metal table, careless of its weight, and had one hand curled into a claw reaching for Tommy.

"Get back!" Tommy screamed at Burns as he hurled a small cart.

The cart cracked Burns in the head, tearing open a wound that wept blood. Burns seemed unconcerned, only grunting and pressing forward.

"Tommy!" Alice yanked his hand, and the two darted toward the hallway.

A wet tendril whipped forward and lashed Tommy across the back, ripping his suit and knocking him forward. Tommy slammed his head into the wall and lost his footing.

"Help me!" Alice screamed at Becks as she grabbed Tommy under his arms.

Becks had been frozen, but now dashed forward, grabbing Tommy. They dragged him as Tommy pushed his feet against the floor to steady himself.

Burns dragged the table across the ground, making it *screech* and leaving a long, trailing scratch mark. His tendrils continued whipping about madly, breaking glass and shattering lights in their frenzy. He came out of the door and bellowed, reaching for Tommy, stopped only by the dragging table caught in the doorway. Screeching over and over again, Burns yanked his wrist until it crunched, snapped, and pulled free from the restraint.

"Someone get a gun!" Becks screamed, still not letting go of Tommy.

Alice's eyes went wide as Burns bore down on them.

---

TEALSON WALKED DOWN toward the belly of the ship. A soft groan of winding metal issued as the gears in his armor turned, adding to his strength. He held his helmet cupped to his hip. He knew the crew wasn't ready for what would come next, but he had to show confidence. He had to let them know there was a plan.

*Earth command has a plan. It's to feed us into the grinder to save someone more important than we are.*

He knew that. It didn't bother him as much as it should have. He'd always been well aware that he was just a cog in the machine.

"Sir!" Tanaka yelled running up behind him. "There's something happening in our med lab. Burns has—"

"Bring my rifle," Tealson snapped off. He didn't need to hear anything else. He pulled the helmet on. It sat in place for a moment before the gears took control and pulled it down tightly.

"*Engaged,*" the armor said as tracking systems lit up in the visor screen in front of him.

Tealson hurried down, taking the stairs like a rampaging elephant. He lost his footing and careened into the wall, putting a dent in it. He shook himself off and made his way toward the med bay, all the while a single thought kept going through his head.

*No one else dies. No one else.*

It was too late now for Burns. He knew that, but if his existence had a purpose, it was to ensure the safety of his crew. He was going to do it with his life if need be.

Barreling into the hallway, he heard the screams before he saw it. Burns was on top of Tommy, terrible, nightmarish tendrils having ripped from his body and snagged around the electrical engineer. Becks was between them, using his forearm on Burns's throat while Alice pulled on Tommy.

Loud, heavy steps reverberated through the whole ship as Tealson closed in. He had no weapon, but he didn't need one.

Not when he could get this close.

"*Move*," he commanded Becks and grabbed Burns by the head. He pulled back, struggling at first as Burns continued to fight, and then the head twisted and snapped, turning from the force of Tealson's strength.

Burns was still moaning, his mouth had turned black and his tongue purple. His eyes were blood red and wide with creeping veins running through them.

The tentacles continued to whip around violently, one tightening around Tommy's neck. Tealson shoved himself between Burns and Tommy, using his hands to grab the tentacle and snap it in half. Putrid yellow and green fluids sprayed out, bathing the walls and Tealson's suit as Becks and Alice dragged off Tommy.

Burns continued fighting weakly against Tealson in the CAG. Bellowing like a ghoul, he raked his fingers against the armor, his nails snapping in a wild attempt to open Tealson like a can of soup.

Tealson pressed him into the floor and then pounded a fist down, feeling the bones in Burns crush with each hit. "Die, dammit!" Tealson screamed after the fifth blow, yet Burns still howled.

The strength of the armor surged through him as Tealson beat Burns, over and over again, amidst the screeching and howling.

After a time, huffing in exhaustion, Tealson stood up from the quivering pile that had once been a member of his crew. Breathing deep and feeling his pulse beat in his ears, Tealson finally turned to Alice.

"What in the fuck just happened?"

ALICE HISSED AIR through a filtered helmet. She swallowed back her fear as the mess that had been Burns continued to quake and spasm.

*Death throes. But be careful.*

Using a scalpel she opened a slit down his chest.

"What the hell is this?" Tealson had asked a short time earlier.

She hadn't known. Nothing about it made sense. She told Tealson as much.

"Then you're going to find out," he'd said. "Open him up."

Now she was performing an autopsy on a broken, shivering body of a man she had played cards with a short time earlier. Several of her crew members were practically looming over her shoulders. Each in CAGs, and each with weapons in hand.

*You don't even know if it's dead.*

That is what ran through her head as she peeled the flesh back, exposing what was left of the ribs.

*The woman in the med lab had no lungs, and no heart. What about Burns?*

A bead of sweat rolled down her cheek. It was irritating, but she hardly noticed it as she rubbed her helmeted face against the back of her wrist.

Curiosity embraced her and pushed her forward, beyond the horrors of the situation. She looked at Burns's ribs and his heart, and the deeper she went, the more she began to understand.

Certain as she could be under the circumstances, she ended the procedure. Burns's body was dumped into a corpse bag and then launched into the void of space.

She reviewed a video of her procedure, trying to determine how best to understand what happened. Finally she came to a conclusion and reported it to Tealson.

"It's not a disease at all. It's a parasite."

The old commander had a hell of a poker face. He was stiff and emotionless. Alice could have been asking him a particularly irritating request for more vacation time by the way he looked.

"How it grew so fast and how it took him is beyond me. But I found this." She held up a jar with what looked like a small kidney, with hundreds of wisps curling out of it. It was partially crushed. "When you smashed it, that's what finally killed it. That's why they don't need a heart, lungs, or even a head. These things go in there and stretch out, puppeting the whole body. At least that's the best conclusion I can come to under the circumstances."

Tealson nodded. He had no other questions. "Dismissed," he told her.

---

TEALSON WALKED INTO LOCKDOWN. He'd made an announcement and told everyone to meet him there. He heard them talking as he made his way in, discussing amongst themselves how they might be going back into cryo. Tanaka was notably quiet.

She already knew.

He looked up and down the line. They were tired. Confused. Afraid.

So was he.

They began to whisper amongst themselves as to *why* he was still in his CAG.

They should have known better.

"I've spoken with Earth Command," Tealson said.

There would be no aborting this mission.

"Our request to abort has been cancelled."

"Oh, *shit*," Elliot hissed, looking like he wanted to run and hide.

The others started to curse and shake their heads, some saying they needed to leave now, others saying that it was useless and everyone was dead.

"No, there was a living woman down there. She was caught in the crossfire, but she proves that *someone* is—or at least *was*—down there alive. That right, Lieutenant Reeves?" Tealson looked to Tommy, who nodded solemnly.

"You heard it, then. Command has passed us down a new mission priority. We are to locate Will Braun. He is a high-priority asset. We need to go in there and retrieve him—"

"He's dead!" Bartlet shouted. *"Everyone's* fucking dead!"

"—or find proof of his death."

"Excuse me," Jeff Regal said, fanning out his arms. "But who the fuck is this guy?"

"Will Braun is Waerheall von Braun," Tealson said. "Repurposed to Mars after his trial."

"No." Parker frowned, tapping his cigar into an ashtray. "He was executed."

"That was the official record, yes," Tealson said.

"Listen," Smith said, shaking his head. "I don't know who the hell Waerheall von Braun is, and I don't give a shit. If he's so valuable, why'd they hide him away out here?"

"Because," Tealson said, looking at Smith, but seeing the other faces of the room. Half of them knew and understood. "He was a Nazi."

Now they all understood.

# EPILOGUE

WILL Braun's breath fogged the window as he looked into space. The ship full of strangers had left Felicity in a haste.

What were the odds that Braun would have looked out at *just* the right moment, at *just* the right angle to see the ship speeding away?

*Highly unlikely.*

The ship had left him to his fate. A long and cold death as the base decompressed, or, possibly, a quick one should the creatures find him.

*No.*

It wasn't going to happen. It was a lie. A cruel joke made against him, as fate smiled to see if it could rattle him. But it didn't. He knew, and he understood.

*This is a lie.*

The men and women around him had moaned, and some beat their hands against the glass in futile attempts to break from the frame that fate had put them in.

Braun would not have such a fate. He was not like them. He would not die in such a place. Not with so much work ahead of him.

"What are we going to do?" someone had asked.

"I'm thinking," Braun had responded. He had been thinking for hours now.

It was not his time. Death would not come for him.

*They need me.*

*The world was a lawless and dangerous place. It needed a guiding hand. A mind to shape the reality they lived in.*

They were cogs in a machine, turning and twisting the passage of time and history. Braun too was a cog.

But he was a particularly large one.

Perhaps the ship had left, and perhaps the crew was gaining some distance now, but it didn't matter.

This would not be his end.

Will Braun no longer had a pulse because he lacked a heart. An engine inside his chest kept the blood flowing. But even if he did have the thumping beat of a heart, he knew his pulse wouldn't have quickened. It would have remained constant, with or without that crew.

No, he wouldn't die here. Of that he was sure.

How long would the life support system hold up? How long would it be until those creatures found the cryo room and made such slumber impossible? He didn't know the answer to these questions, but he knew it meant all the world to the others breathing around him. It meant little to him.

*I won't die here.*

All the others were vulnerable. Each fragile and moments away from shattering.

It was time to plan, for the sake of the fragile existence of the others. Was cryo the only option? How could any of them feel safe going into cryosleep with those abominations lurking about the base? He glanced down at the pipe wrench he'd wielded as a makeshift weapon and laughed—a dry, harsh sound that rattled in his throat and fell on deaf ears. The other scientists shot a volley of questions in his direction, mostly about the identity of their would-be rescuers, as if he had any more information than the rest of them.

"Orbital Corps recon team, most likely," he'd said. "Scrubs. Pawns. Go-boys. Whatever you want to call them. It doesn't matter. They're gone now."

Some of them had taken to crying, to hopeless theatrics. Asking God for help. Asking God *why*.

Of course, he'd heard it all before—many, many times. He heard it on a daily basis for years, walking past the groups of tired, terrified faces. He'd heard their cries to God. Their pleas to the guards, the soldiers. To anyone who would listen to what they had to say.

Waerheall von Braun, he'd gone by back then. Those were simpler times, back when he had a clear objective, a job to be done in the service of his country.

Für Deutschland.

Für die Zukunft.

Für den Führer.

He'd since traded one country for another, but the good work continued. He took a deep breath of stale, recycled air and stared out into the vast reaches of space.

He thought back on all the terrible things he'd witnessed during his duties as a scientist for the Third Reich. Certainly he'd contributed to the pain and suffering of many poor souls, it was the reason he'd been moved to Felicity in the first place. It was one thing for America to employ one of the world's brightest minds to help in the war effort against the Russians, but it was another thing entirely to employ a *Nazi*.

*Oh, the horror.*

Nobody cared. So the United States did what they did best. They brushed it under the rug, hiding him away on a completely different planet. Of course, the story had been that he'd been executed.

*But this is where I was needed.*

That was what he reminded himself of in his weaker moments, when he started to doubt fate, but he knew it was true. *He was needed here.* The things they had discovered here while on Mars, the *progress* they had made—it was because of *him*.

It was the reason why they couldn't really leave him there to die. It's why he knew this was all just a cruel joke of fate to see if he would crack.

He wouldn't.

Stepping close to the window once more, he looked out.

And what were the odds, at that moment, from this angle. . . he would see the ship returning.

As it re-entered the Martian atmosphere he felt a laugh erupting from somewhere deep within, a rumbling, cascading sound that shook him to his very core.

"Pathetic," he said between laughs. "Absolutely pathetic."

He stared at his reflection in the glass, feeling less human than ever before.

*I should be happy they're coming back. I should feel something.*

His reflection seemed to taunt him, reminding him that he was barely alive. Cold. Mechanical. Picking up the pipe wrench, he toyed with it between his hands before smashing it into his reflection in a blind rage, cracking the glass in a spider-web pattern so he could no longer see his own face looking back at him.

*There. . . that's better.*

# MORE CONTENT

Continue reading for the following extra content:

- Bonus Epilogue: *Earth Command.*
- Staff information: *Logs of the Perihelion*
- History of the World: *The Cold War*

And join Reality Bleed's exclusive discussion group to talk about the book with other readers!

Hope to see you there.

- Winter Gate Publishing

# EARTH COMMAND

Want to know more of Richard John Roles of Earth Command?
Join our mailing list for this bonus epilogue.
Get it at: **https://tinyurl.com/EarthCommand**

# LOGS OF THE PERIHELION

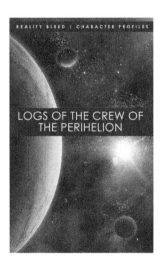

Go to **https://tinyurl.com/CrewLogs** to get this free bonus book and learn more of the Crew of the Perihelion.

# BONUS CONTENT

The following is bonus content added for readers interested in knowing more about the world of Reality Bleed. It is not *required reading* but is only here as an add on.

We hope you enjoy it.

# THE COLD WAR

RICHIE RUBBED the back of his head and yawned. He had about an hour's worth of studying left to do, but his brain was already mush.

"Drink this, it'll put hair on your nads," his friend had said as he'd slapped down an energy drink on the table in front of him.

Richie had chugged it two hours ago, and though he wasn't sure it'd increase the hair count on his body, it had boosted him. . . for a while, anyway.

Now he was crashing—hard.

"*Shit.*" He yawned again as he looked away from his books, feeling like the stack was staring him down, judging him for not working harder.

*I'll just take a break and watch a video, then get back to work.*

It rarely worked that way. As soon as he started playing internet videos, he often fell down some strange rabbit hole until he found himself watching machine presses smashing things, or weird reaction videos to things he cared nothing about.

He saw the icon then with the message: *Is the Cold War Heating Up?*

That would be at least sort-of productive, wouldn't it? It'd certainly help with his history class.

"Sure, why not?" he said to no one in particular as he leaned back in his chair and moused over the video.

Click.

An icon spun in the middle of the screen, and then the video loaded. A man in a black suit with a white dress shirt sat casually at a desk, looking directly into the camera. His tie had been loosened to make it more comfortable. He was thin with a beard and in one hand he held a smoldering cigarette.

*Well ain't this guy a badass.*

Richie half-snorted and moved the mouse to close the video but stopped when the man started talking.

"The problem today," the man said, "is that young people don't understand our history. They don't understand the *Cold War*." White text flashed on the bottom of the screen which read: *Dr. Jordan Robertson, Clinical Psychologist and Historian.*

Richie leaned back, deciding not to close the video. There was something in the man's voice, a look on his face. The seriousness.

The man held the cigarette to his lips and puffed it down, exhaling a stream of smoke through his nose. "They hear stories about a butchered girl in the West and think, *Comanche uprising.* They hear of the occupation of Libya and see it as a failed war we should have never been in." He tipped his hand and pointed directly at the camera, his cigarette sizzling between two fingers. "They don't understand the *game* we're in. They don't understand that the struggles of the *Great Powers* shape the world."

*Holy shit.*

Richie leaned in, putting his elbows on the table and setting his chin down on his crossed arms.

The man went on. "It's move," the man pointed at one side of his desk, and then the other. "And counter move." He took another puff. "When does the world burn? That's my question to you." He pointed his fingers at the camera again. *"When does it burn?"*

Richie's dorm room door opened and he hit pause on the video. "Hey," Richie said.

His roommate, Jeff, nodded his head and threw his coat on his bed. "Sup?"

"Come here, you have to see this." Richie waved him over.

"What is it?" Jeff huffed as he dropped his backpack on the floor with a *thud*. "I got shit to do."

"Just look at this guy, he's intense."

Jeff walked over and hunched over to see the screen as Richie hit the play button.

"The Cold War looms over us, but we don't even talk about it anymore." He held two fingers out like a gun and stuck it to his head. "Aim a gun to a man's head and he'll panic. Keep it there for sixty years and he won't even notice it anymore." Jordan let his thumb click down like the hammer on a revolver. "The *Cold War* gets hot."

"What the hell is this guy talking about?" Jeff asked as he took a seat.

"Just watch," Richie told him.

Jordan leaned back in his chair, breathing deep as if to collect his thoughts. "It's nineteen fourty seven. World War two has just ended. Japan is split in half, North and South. Berlin is laid to waste with two atomic bombs, and all of Germany is likewise, cut in half. Is the *Cold War* hot?" Jordan shrugged his shoulders.

Jeff pointed at the screen, "This guy needs to either smoke more, or less weed, I can't tell which."

Richie snorted.

"It's nineteen fifty six," Jordan said. "Time magazine publishes a picture, showing the corpse of Japanese woman who'd just made the attempt to cross into Southern Japan before she was gunned down. Her dead eyes are whispered about across America. Is the *Cold War* hot?"

The image of the woman flashed across the screen. She looked oddly unconcerned, but her eyes were wide. Richie might have thought she was alive, if not for the blood covering her chest and up toward her neck.

"*Fuck*," Richie hissed, the image had caught him by surprise.

"Shit, I don't want to see that," Jeff said, but made no attempt to leave or turn the video off.

Jordan's cigarette burned orange as he puffed. He took it out and looked at it, then snuffed it into an ashtray. It smoldered as he talked. "It's now the fifties. Two American turncoats sell the plans to make nuclear weapons to the Soviets. Southeastern Asian alliance is formed. When Korea attempts to leave, some five years later, Chinese forces occupy the peninsula. An insurgent war continues to this day."

More images pop up. One is of a smiling Chinese man pointing up to a post with three bodies hanging from it. Another is of three young men, standing in a line, each with a Korean flag sewn to their coats, holding their rifles over their heads and screaming.

The last image is of a young girl, crying and holding her baby brother.

They're both completely naked.

Richie rubs the side of his head, but only because he's trying hard not to let his eyes go red. The last picture was so *alive*, he could almost hear the girl screaming.

"There has never been a time in human history when a weapon's system has been developed and not utilized. *Never.*" Jordan held out both of his hands. "*Until* now. America acquired nuclear weapons first. The Soviet Union shortly after. The Asian alliance a little later. And finally, shortly after its formation in the nineteen nineties, so did the European Federation. A man said, '*You may reasonably expect a man to walk a tightrope safely for ten minutes. It would be unreasonable to do so without accident for two hundred years.*'"

Jordan cracked a nihilistic grin. "How long can the *Cold War* stay *cold* with all those weapons out there? How many," he held up two fingers on each hand and curled them in air quotes, "*incidents* can we expect before a world ending exchange of weapons finishes us all?" He shrugged, one corner of his mouth smugly raised. "'I'm not a betting man, but I wouldn't say *long*. We're currently living in the age of the insurgent. Where the great powers cannot afford any direct confrontation, so we meddle with each other's affairs in secret, with bribes, weapons, and intelligence. It's a fun game we all play, and you know it's a game because there are rules. The rules are—" he slammed a fist into an open hand. "—pound the hell out of any smaller country that might favor one of your enemies. Do whatever you'd like to them, just make sure you don't cross this invisible line we've drawn somewhere, but hey, we also forgot where we drew the line." Jordan shrugged again. "What's too much? Was it when Americans started supplying weapons to Ukranian separatist? Or was it when the Soviets began failing in the face of the space race so they *accidentally* shot down an American cargo ship? How about when those Libyan terrorists bombed the state's building, and the sequential *failed* invasion and occupation of Libya? Presumably armed by the Soviets, because hey, Libyans don't just build AK-47's by themselves do they?"

Smirking, Jordan began to tick off facts. "It's the nineteen seventies and Afghan jihadists blow up a Soviet Emissary in Saudi Arabia, prompting a long back and forth with the countries eventually leading to a Soviet invasion. Americans supply the Afghans. Now the Soviets are occupying Ukraine, Afghanistan, and North Japan, as well as supplying weapons to their allies in the Asian Alliance to subdue separatist. They feel the need to respond, and just as America is pulling out of Libya, hey, wouldn't you know it, there are some Comanche that have a bone to pick. Surprise, surprise, who knew those guys were still around? Now it's certainly conjecture to say the Soviets supply them, but hey, do you think Comanche can just *up* and cook nerve gas on their own?"

A short video played that showed row after row of bodies in bags. A man in a chemical suit walks past them, his head down and shaking from side to side.

The video snapped back to Jordan. "Is the *Cold War* hot?" He exhaled and stared at the camera. "Step by step, we walk toward Armageddon. Each move on the checkerboard brings us all closer to the *endgame*. We are now in a situation where The Soviet Union has supplied weapons directly toward enemies *inside* the United States. Now has this—" he pointed a finger down and waved it in front of him. "imaginary line been crossed? Are we now to find enemies directly in the Soviet Union and supply them with the next step above nerve agents? Is it wise to keep playing this *game?*" He shrugged again and laughed. "Hell, I don't know. It's just that—

Richie paused the video and leaned back.

"Why'd you pause it?" Jeff asked him. "Dude is on a roll. Giving me chills with his whole *Is the Cold War Hot? Ahh!*" Jeff mocked Jordan's voice.

"I don't know man. It's giving me some weird ass feelings." Richie shook his head.

"What do you mean?"

"The Russians. They *do* have their nukes pointed at us."

Jeff snorted. "So? Who gives a shit."

Richie turned and looked out the window. "Can you imagine just looking out there one day and seeing the mushroom cloud? You'd almost rather it be close enough to kill you rather than survive in the fall out. That would—"

"Shit man," Jeff stood up and slapped him on the shoulder. "I think *you* either need to start smoking more or less weed."

Richie laughed as Jeff walked away. He looked back at the screen. He knew he really should start studying.

But he was drawn in.

He clicked the video again.

# WHAT'S NEXT?

Want to know the latest on the *Reality Bleed* series?

Join our Facebook group to talk *Reality Bleed* and keep up-to-date on everything that's happening.

# CALL OF THE VOID

## REALITY BLEED BOOK 2

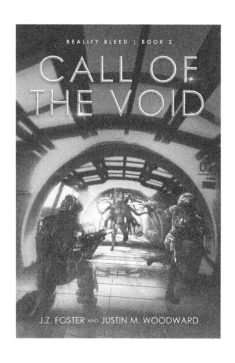

# CRASH. BURN. DIE.

## REALITY BLEED BOOK 3

# NIGHT TERRORS

## REALITY BLEED BOOK 4

# ABOUT J.Z. FOSTER

J.Z. Foster is a writer originally from Ohio. He spent several years in South Korea where he met and married his wife.

He received the writing bug from his mother, NYTimes best-selling author, Lori Foster.

Check out his other books and let him know how you like them!

Write him an email at:
*JZFoster@JZFoster.com*

# ABOUT JUSTIN M. WOODWARD

Justin M. Woodward is an author from Headland, Alabama. He lives with his wife and two small boys. He has been writing since 2015.

He's had stories appear in various anthologies alongside authors like Stephen King and Neil Gaiman. His work has been featured in Scream Magazine.

You can keep up with him on social media, and on www.justinm-woodward.com

WINTER GATE PUBLISHING

Want to stay up to date on the latest from Winter Gate Publishing?
Follow us on Facebook at Facebook.com/WinterGatePublishing to
know more!

Winter Gate Publishing. Reality Bleed: Hell on Mars

Made in the USA
Monee, IL
05 March 2024

54508175R00094